"I suppose yo
appointment
Liam said flat

Clearly he wasn't a̶n̶y̶ ̶m̶o̶r̶e̶ ̶p̶l̶e̶a̶s̶e̶d̶ ̶w̶i̶t̶h̶ ̶t̶h̶i̶s̶
surprise turn of events than she was.

She nodded. "Yes. The senior pastor hired me over the phone. I'm the new ballet teacher."

Ballet teacher. The words tasted like sand in her mouth.

"*Temporary* ballet teacher," she added for clarification. She wanted to make sure that was clear from the very beginning. "I'm only in town for six weeks."

How things had changed over the course of five short days. She was back here in Alaska, where the snow was real, where bears took naps and where her new boss was her old love. She could still hear the echo of that horrifying crack in her foot.

Once her foot healed, she was going back to San Francisco. Gabriel had promised not to make a final decision about who would be promoted to principal until the parts in *Firebird* had been cast. She still had one last chance.

A small one, to be sure, but she wasn't giving up without a fight.

Teri Wilson grew up as an only child and could often be found with her head in a book, lost in a world of heroes, heroines and exotic places. As an adult, her love of books has led her to her dream career—writing. Teri's other passions include dance and travel. She lives in Texas, and loves to hear from readers. Teri can be contacted via her website, teriwilson.net.

Books by Teri Wilson

Love Inspired

Alaskan Hearts
Alaskan Hero
Sleigh Bell Sweethearts
Alaskan Homecoming

Visit the Author Profile page at Harlequin.com for more titles

Alaskan Homecoming

Teri Wilson

HARLEQUIN® LOVE INSPIRED®

Recycling programs
for this product may
not exist in your area.

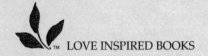 LOVE INSPIRED BOOKS

ISBN-13: 978-0-373-87947-2

Alaskan Homecoming

www.Harlequin.com

Printed in U.S.A.

A time to weep and a time to laugh,
a time to mourn and a time to dance.
—*Ecclesiastes* 3:4

For Crystal,
my favorite ballerina

Acknowledgments

Many thanks to Crystal Serrano for her expert
ballet knowledge and for making my legs shake
in barre class; Elizabeth Winick Rubinstein and
everyone at McIntosh & Otis; Rachel Burkot,
Melissa Endlich and the wonderful staff
at Harlequin Books; my critique partner,
Meg Benjamin; and my family and friends
for their unwavering support.

And as always, I thank God
for making my dreams come true
and allowing me to write for a living.

Chapter One

Be still. Do not move a muscle. And whatever you do, don't scream.

Posy Sutton bit her lip to prevent the forbidden scream from slipping out. She wanted very much to yell for help at the top of her lungs. Who wouldn't, standing there with an awkward plaster cast on her foot and looking at what was a mere ten feet in front of her?

A bear.

From the looks of its wooly brown backside, a brown bear. Or possibly a grizzly, which, as bears went, was the very worst sort to bump into. Not that a brown bear would be a picnic.

Don't do it. Don't scream.

Posy might have been back in her hometown of Aurora, Alaska, for only a matter of hours, but she was no cheechako—Alaska's common nickname for newcomers. She'd grown up here. Six years in San Francisco couldn't erase the lessons she'd had drilled into her as a child. She knew how to behave around bears in the wilderness—*avoid eye contact, do not scream or yell. If the bear doesn't see you, walk away very slowly. If the bear does see you, play dead.*

The problem was that she wasn't exactly in the wilderness at the moment. In fact, she wasn't outdoors at all. She was standing in the fellowship hall of Aurora Community Church. All alone. There wasn't another soul in sight.

Unless the bear whose tail end was currently sticking out of the overturned trash can in the corner was to be counted. Bears had souls, didn't they?

Posy rolled her eyes. Now wasn't exactly the time to contemplate the eternal salvation of Smokey, Paddington and the like.

The bear grunted, its rumbling voice echoing from within the metal trash can. It sounded so…so…*sinister.* And hungry. Very hungry. Like every growling stomach in the universe all rolled into one. Posy's heart thumped so hard, she thought it might beat right out of her chest. She'd never been so terrified in her life. Not even the first time she'd danced the role of Clara in *The Nutcracker* as a ten-year-old. Nor opening night of her debut as a soloist with the West Coast Arts Ballet Company, plucked from the corps de ballet and thrust directly into the spotlight.

She was standing in an enclosed space with a grizzly. And she was on crutches. Could it get any worse?

One sound, one telltale movement and the bear would realize she was there. And she'd be taken down like a weak zebra on the National Geographic Channel.

She tightened her grip on her crutches and took a deep, calming breath, much like the one she always took in the final seconds before the red velvet curtains parted on performance nights. Only this breath wasn't all that calming. Her chest grew tighter. She thought she might be hyperventilating. She prayed for a paper bag. Or better yet, a can of bear repellent.

Bear repellent.

Posy hadn't seen a can of bear spray in years. San Francisco wasn't without its dangers, but bears didn't exactly make the short list. Or the long list. Or any variation of the list whatsoever. Bear repellent was obviously no longer a staple in her handbag. But hair spray certainly was. Ballerina buns didn't stay put on their own.

Without taking her eyes off the bear's broad, furry hindquarters, she anchored her right crutch firmly under her arm and reached into her purse for the can of Aqua Net that she never went anywhere without. Okay, so it wasn't exactly Mace for wild animals, but maybe it would do in a pinch. As carefully and quietly as she could manage, she pried off the lid. But her hands were shaking so badly that it fell to the ground before she could catch it.

To Posy's ears, it sounded louder than a gunshot when it hit the tile floor and bounced what had to be at least a dozen times. The world came to an abrupt standstill. Save for the lid to the Aqua Net clattering around like a pinball, nothing moved. Not Posy. Not the dust in the air. Not even the bear. All rummaging had ceased. Not a muscle moved in that furry back end, until the bear slowly began walking backward, extricating itself from the trash can.

Oh no, oh no, oh no, oh no.

Posy took an instinctive step backward with her left foot. The injured one. Pain shot through her plaster cast, and she stumbled. One crutch clattered to the ground. She seized on to the other with both desperate hands and teetered sideways. The crutch wobbled. And the tile floor suddenly seemed to be rising up to meet her. Just as she realized she was going down, the bear shot the rest of the way out of the trash can in a fuzzy brown blur.

Posy screamed. She no longer cared about the rules. If she was about to become bear chow, someone somewhere was going to hear about it. Her scream echoed off the walls of the fellowship hall as she tumbled to the ground.

Then, before her body made contact with the hard tile, she was lifted into the air from behind by a powerful force.

Her terror grew tenfold. And her first thought was that she was being tag teamed. By bears.

Well, she wasn't going down without a fight. She had only one weapon left at her disposal, and she didn't hesitate to use it. She pressed down on the Aqua Net nozzle as hard as she could and aimed the can over her shoulder, screaming all the while.

"Ouch! What the…"

The talking bear—*talking bear?*—released its hold on her and she toppled to the floor, landing squarely on her backside, which was good. She didn't mind a bruised behind as long as she didn't reinjure her foot. Assuming she wasn't about to be eaten, she needed that foot to heal in time for the spring production of *Firebird*.

"What was that for?"

Posy glanced up at the figure towering over her.

A man. Not another bear.

A man.

A man pressing the heels of his hands into his puffy red eyes and groaning as though he'd been doused with pepper spray or something.

Posy glanced at the can of Aqua Net still clutched in her hand. Great. Just great. Someone had actually come to her aid, and she'd maced him.

"I'm sorry. I didn't mean to spray you. I meant to spray him." She pointed toward the bear, which had extricated itself from the trash can and was now spinning happy circles chasing its tail.

Posy stared at it. That didn't seem like normal bear behavior. And now that she got a good look at the creature, it looked less like a bear and more like a…

"My dog?" the man barked. "You wanted to spray my dog with hair spray?"

"Yes." She scrambled rather inelegantly to her feet, gathering up her crutches along the way. "I mean, no."

"Which is it? Yes or no? Me or the dog?" He sounded angry. Angrier than a mama bear defending her cub.

Not that Posy could blame him. She'd had an eyeful of Aqua Net on more than one occasion, particularly in her early years with the dance company when she'd shared a cramped dressing room with every one of the other thirteen members of the corps. It wasn't pleasant.

She forced herself to tear her gaze away from the dog. Not such an easy task. It was an enormous, hulking beast. Very bearlike in appearance, other than the lolling tongue and great swinging tail. She kept doing double takes to make sure it was, in fact, a dog. It let out a woof, and she finally felt safe enough to take her eyes off it.

"Again, I'm sorry. Very sorry." Her cheeks flared with heat. "I thought your dog was a bear."

He removed his hands from his face and looked down at her with incredulous eyes. Red, puffy, incredulous eyes.

Posy lost her balance for a moment, then righted herself. She found it difficult to breathe all of a sudden.

She stared at the man, sure she was hallucinating. A name—*the* name—from her past echoed in her ears, along with the pounding of her suddenly out-of-control pulse.

Liam.

No. It couldn't be. It looked like him—same charmingly rumpled dark hair, same broad shoulders, same chiseled jaw. Except now those shoulders seemed even broader, the jaw more finely sculpted and covered with a dark shadow of masculine stubble. Six years was a long time. Long enough to change a boy into a man, apparently.

"Posy?" he said, the shock she felt down to her core mirrored in his expression.

And for the briefest of moments she was eighteen again, living in a snow-globe world of young love, cozy Alaskan winters and wild-heartbeat romance. Laughter. Long walks among snow-laden evergreens. The thrill of her frosty first kiss while swirling snowflakes gathered in her hair.

She swallowed. "Liam."

His name felt somehow both familiar and foreign on her tongue. Like a favorite thick, cozy cardigan sweater that looked the same as it always had, but no longer seemed to fit once you slipped it on.

"Posy," he said again, a coldness creeping into his voice.

She opened her mouth to say something, anything, but then Liam's gaze dropped lower. To her foot. And the ugly anchor attached to it—her plaster cast.

Breathe. Just breathe.

Without even realizing what she was doing, she closed her eyes. Only five days had passed since her injury, but that was long enough for Posy to grow more than weary of the looks of pity that the chunk of plaster elicited from people who knew she was a ballerina. It was like walking around with your biggest inadequacy on display for all the world to see.

If Liam looked at her with even the smallest amount of pity in his gaze, the brave front she'd been putting on for the past five days just might crumble to pieces. Dancing had taught her a lot of things—determination, discipline, how to tolerate pain. But it hadn't prepared her for this: coming face-to-face with her past.

With Liam Blake. The last person in Alaska she wanted to see.

Truth be told, she much preferred the idea of a run-in with a grizzly.

Posy Sutton.

Liam blinked. His eyes burned like a wildfire, and his vision was still a bit fuzzy, but even through the fog of hair spray he could see that familiar swan neck, those long, graceful limbs, those huge, haunted eyes.

Posy Sutton.

With a cast on her foot.

She was injured. Of course. Why else would she have come back? She'd danced away from Alaska as quickly as she could. He should have known there was a reason she'd returned. A reason that had nothing whatsoever to do with the past. With him.

Get over yourself. It was six years ago. She's moved on. You've moved on.

He ground his teeth. He might have moved on, but that didn't mean he had to ask about her foot. Or how it was affecting her dancing. If he so much as uttered the word *ballet*, he might sound like a jealous lover. Posy may have been his first love, but dance had been hers.

Her first love. Her only love. She'd sacrificed everything for it.

He'd never stood a chance.

He forced his gaze away from the cast. He'd seen a cast on the very same foot before. That first cast had been what started it all. The beginning of the end. He'd felt sorry for her then, which was how he'd let things get so out of hand. In the end, he'd done the right thing, and she'd never forgiven him. In a single bittersweet moment, he'd saved her and lost her at the same time.

If she expected sympathy from him now, she was in for a big disappointment. He'd been down that road before and had no intention of traveling that way again. He jammed his hands on his hips and paid no attention to the cast or the crutches she seemed to be struggling to keep from sliding out from under her.

The injury must be recent.

He chastised himself for wondering about it, pretended not to notice the foot and refocused on her face. Her eyes were closed for some strange reason. He pretended not to notice that, as well. "You thought my dog was a bear?"

"I did." Her lashes fluttered open, and she met his gaze. Full-on eye contact.

Those eyes. Those luminous eyes, the exact color of a stormy winter sea. Misty gray. He'd never forgotten those eyes, no matter how hard he'd tried.

He cleared his throat. "Well, he's not. He's a dog."

As if on cue, Sundog abandoned chasing his tail and bounded over to the two of them. Posy's eyes grew wide, and she teetered backward on her crutches. By the look on her face, anyone would have thought the dog was about to rise up on its hind legs, grizzly-style, and tear her limb from limb.

Liam reached out to keep her from falling. Again. "Careful there."

"I'm fine." She wiggled out of his reach. "Thank you, but I'm fine."

Fine.

She was fine. He was fine. They were all fine.

Except not really. This whole encounter was as awkward as it could be, and it somehow seemed to be getting worse by the minute.

"What kind of dog is he, anyway? He's as big as a…"

"Bear?" Liam asked, grinning despite himself.

She offered him a hesitant smile in return. "I was going to say 'house,' but 'bear' works. Obviously."

"He's a Newfoundland." He watched Posy reach out a tentative hand and stroke Sundog's head.

Never in his wildest dreams did he imagine he'd one day be standing in church while a very adult Posy Sutton petted his dog. It didn't seem real. He almost felt as if he was watching a movie about someone else's life.

And what if it had been someone else? What would Liam say to the man standing there with puffy eyes? The man who suddenly had the beginnings of a smile on his face?

Don't be an idiot. What's past is past.

That was precisely what he would say.

He cleared his throat. "It's the dead of winter. Bears are hibernating."

"What?" Posy's hand paused over Sundog's massive head.

"You thought you saw a bear." Liam shrugged. "Not possible. They're all tucked in for winter."

Her brow furrowed. "Oh, that's right. I guess I forgot."

After a prolonged beat of silence, Liam crossed his arms. "I'm sure there are a great number of things you've forgotten. You've been gone a long time."

She flinched a little. Her stormy eyes narrowed. "Six years. Not that long."

He lifted a brow. "Long enough to forget that bears hibernate." What self-respecting Alaskan didn't know that?

But that was precisely the point, wasn't it? Posy hadn't been an Alaskan for quite a while. In truth, Liam envied her. Not because she'd left, but because she'd forgotten. There were plenty of things he'd like to forget.

Her cheeks flushed pink. "The bears are sleeping. Duly noted." Her tone had gone colder than a glacier.

She was angry. Good. So was he. Why exactly, he wasn't quite sure. But he had a feeling it had less to do with his stinging eyes than it did Posy's sudden reappearance in their hometown.

His hometown. He was the one who loved it here. He was the one who'd stayed.

"So when did you get back?" If forced to guess, he would have said a day. Two, tops. Any longer than that, and he would have heard about it. Someone would have seen her and run to him with the news. Over half a decade had passed since they'd been high school sweethearts, but small towns like Aurora had long memories.

At the change of subject, her expression softened. Just

a bit. "I came in with Bill Warren this afternoon on his mail run from Anchorage."

"I see."

He didn't see. Not really. As one of only a handful of small-aircraft pilots in Aurora, Bill made a daily jaunt to Anchorage on behalf of the postal service. He never flew up there until after lunch, to be sure the mail was ready. Everyone in Aurora knew the drill.

Liam glanced at his watch. Three o'clock, which meant Posy had been back in town less than an hour. And her first stop was church? That seemed odd.

He started to ask her if he could point her in the direction of the prayer room or the senior pastor's office, in case she was lost. If she thought there were bears in the trash cans, it wasn't such a big leap to think she might have forgotten her way around, even though they'd spent a fair amount of time in this place as teenagers. In this very room, now that he thought about it.

"Listen." He cleared his throat. "I've got some things to do around here. Can I help you find someone?"

He still had an hour or so before the kids showed up after school. But he had an appointment on his calendar with an actual grown-up, a rarity since he spent most of his time with teenagers. A grown-up who he hoped would be the answer to his prayers—a long-awaited assistant for the after-school program.

"Oh. Well, thank you for the rescue, and I apologize again for macing you. I'm sure you have someplace you need to be." She just stood there on her crutches, as if waiting for him to leave.

"Actually, right here is where I need to be." He tucked his hands into his pockets, unease snaking its way up his spine.

He'd been so thrown by seeing her that he hadn't thought

to wonder why she was there in the first place. *No. No, it can't be. It just can't.*

Posy grew very still, as if contemplating the same uncomfortable possibility that was running through his head. "You followed your big unruly dog in here, right? That's the only reason you're here."

She stated it as fact, as if any other possibility was a thought too horrifying to consider.

He gave his head a slow shake.

She swallowed. Liam's eyes traced the movement up and down the slender column of her throat. She was elegance personified. She always had been. Those willowy limbs. Her every movement so fluid that she gave the impression she was made of liquid instead of flesh and bone. She didn't just look like a swan. She *was* a swan.

"My dog might be big, but he's not unruly," he said.

Posy rolled her eyes. "He knocked over a trash can and ate half its contents."

"He's on a diet. It's a recent thing." Why were they making what amounted to small talk and avoiding the issue at hand?

Because I know what's going on here, and I don't like it. Not one bit.

"Why are you here, Posy?" he asked.

He knew the answer before she even opened her mouth.

"I work here," she said warily.

A pain sprang into existence somewhere in Liam's head. "You work here?"

He'd been asking the senior pastor to hire an assistant for the after-school program for months. There was a new city grant up for grabs, and with a little help, the youth program at the church might prove a worthy recipient. It would mean winter coats for those kids he'd noticed who were still wearing last year's threadbare hand-me-downs. It would mean computers and internet for the teens who couldn't afford such luxuries at home. How it meant that he would be working alongside Posy was a mystery.

What was happening?

He lifted his gaze briefly to the ceiling. *Really, Lord?*

"Yes. I'm looking for my new boss. The youth pastor. You don't know where he is, do you?" She looked around as if waiting for someone else, anyone else, to materialize out of thin air.

Oh, how Liam wished someone would. "I'm afraid you're looking at him."

She shook her head, clearly unwilling or unable to believe him.

I'm not any happier about this than you are, darling.

"Liam, if this is your idea of a joke, it's really not funny," she said. Her voice shook a little. Nerves? Anger?

He wasn't sure. It came as somewhat of a shock that he no longer knew what was going on in her head simply by reading her pretty face. It shouldn't have. But it did.

He swallowed. "Do I look like I'm laughing?"

Chapter Two

There had to be some mistake.

"You're the youth pastor?" she asked, praying she'd somehow misunderstood. Of all the people in Alaska, Liam couldn't be her new boss. He just couldn't.

Her mother was the one who'd told her about the job. *Her mother.* And she hadn't thought to mention that Liam was the youth pastor?

"Yep. I'm the youth pastor." He folded his arms and nodded. "Did you think I still worked at the pond?"

The pond. Aurora's skating rink. It was like something out of a Snoopy cartoon—a small, oblong-shaped patch of ice surrounded by thick snowbanks, evergreens and a collection of spindly trees, their bare branches piled with snow. Back when she was in high school, you could rent skates for a dollar a day. Paper cups of hot chocolate with marshmallows had cost even less. Music was played on an old jam box turned up as high as it could go. All during eleventh and twelfth grade Liam had worked there, zipping around the rink on his black skates, making sure everyone followed the rules and no one got hurt. A referee of sorts.

"Did I think you still worked at the pond? Don't be silly. No, of course not." Never in a million years would she admit that when she thought of him, he still zipped through her imagination on those skates. Never in a million years would she admit that she still thought about him period. Because that was just pathetic.

She wasn't a starry-eyed teenager anymore. She was a twenty-four-year-old woman with a real career who lived in one of the most exciting cities in the country. In the world, even. Opportunity had been spread at her feet like a blanket of untouched wildflowers. Since she'd left Aurora, life had been hers for the taking. The most significant romance of her life shouldn't still be the boy who'd asked her to the high school prom.

Then why was it?

Being a ballet dancer didn't leave much time for dating. It didn't leave much time for a life. The few men she'd actually gone out with hadn't stuck around for long. Probably because she canceled or postponed more dates than she actually went on. Somehow heading out for a night on the town after an entire day of dance classes and rehearsals sounded more exhausting than fun. And when performance season was under way, forget it. The only things she looked forward to at the end of those nights were ice baths.

But she was happy. She was living the life she'd always wanted.

Her foot throbbed in the plaster cast. She stared at it as if it belonged to another person. Her foot didn't belong in there. It belonged in a pointe shoe of shiny pink satin. Her foot didn't belong there, and she didn't belong here. In the church of her childhood. The church where Liam was currently the youth pastor.

It's only temporary. Just until the foot heals.

But if Liam was the youth pastor, that meant he was her temporary boss.

She needed a minute—or a century—for that to sink in. Posy had known things in Aurora would be different now. She wasn't delusional. Time hadn't stood still while she'd been away. And Liam's father had been a clergyman—a circuit preacher who traveled to the most remote parts of Alaska to tend to his flock. As far as Posy knew, he was still a traveling preacher. So it shouldn't have come as a total surprise that Liam had followed a similar path.

Although he'd never been that crazy about his dad's calling when they'd been teenagers. In fact, he'd had a pretty large chip on his shoulder about it.

No matter where Liam worked, she'd assumed she'd be in town for at least a day or two before she'd come face-to-face with him. While she was debating whether or not to come home, she'd even managed to convince herself that she might not run into him at all. Aurora was a small town, but she'd come back to teach ballet. And if there was one thing Liam hated, it was ballet.

"Is there another youth pastor, maybe?" She prayed there was. But even as she was silently pleading with God for a second youth pastor to materialize out of thin air, Liam's head was shaking.

"No. Just me, the one and only."

The one and only. Posy took a slow, measured breath. *Seriously, God? Is this Your idea of a joke?*

What had she possibly done to deserve this? First she'd broken her foot on opening night. Not just any opening night, but the most important opening night of her dance career. She'd been cast as the Winter Fairy in *Cinderella*, one of the most coveted roles in the entire production. The principal ballerina had been dancing the role of Cinderella, naturally. The leading parts were always danced by the principals, which was why Posy wanted nothing more than to be a principal herself. It was what every dancer in every ballet company wanted. Members of the corps de ballet dreamed of it. Soloists dreamed of it. Every ballerina did.

Every ballerina did, but only the tiniest percentage of

ballerinas saw those dreams come to fruition. Only the best of the best. The charmed few. And Posy's dance career was looking awfully charmed.

Or it had been, anyway.

The principal dancer cast as Cinderella was retiring. It would be her final role, which meant the company would need a new lead ballerina. The obvious choice would be for Gabriel, the director of the company, to promote either of the two soloists. Posy was one of those soloists, which meant she had a fifty-fifty shot. All she had to do was really nail her performance as the Winter Fairy in all twelve performances of *Cinderella* and she was sure she'd be the one chosen. She'd wanted this for her entire life, since she'd slipped on her first pair of pale pink, buttery-leather ballet slippers. She was ready. It was her turn.

And then right as she'd lifted herself up for her first arabesque exactly as she'd done so many times before in rehearsal, she heard a crack. It was so loud she could hear it above the strains of the orchestra playing Prokofiev's dramatic score. At first she thought a part of the set must have collapsed. Maybe something had fallen from one of the rafters backstage. But deep down, she knew it wasn't that sort of sound. This sound was unique to the human body, a body that was breaking down. Her body. It was the sound of a bone cracking in two. She knew it even before her ankle gave way and she went tumbling to the floor.

Opening night. Her big chance. And it had ended in the first ten seconds. She should have been dancing her way to a promotion, but instead she was lying in a heap onstage, snowflakes falling softly on her from the rafters. Not real snow, of course. Theatrical snow.

And now she was here. In Alaska, where the snow was real, where bears took naps and where her new boss was her old love. How things had changed over the course of five short days. She could swear she still heard the echo of that horrifying crack in her foot.

"I suppose you're the appointment I'm expecting?" Liam said flatly. Clearly he wasn't any more pleased with this surprise turn of events than she was.

She nodded. "Yes. The senior pastor hired me over the phone. I'm the new ballet teacher."

Ballet teacher. The words tasted like sand in her mouth.

"*Temporary* ballet teacher," she added for clarification. She wanted to make sure that was clear from the very beginning. "I'm only in town for six weeks."

Once her foot healed, she was going back to San Francisco. Gabriel had promised not to make a final decision about who would be promoted to principal until the parts in *Firebird* had been cast. She still had one last chance. A small one, to be sure, but she wasn't giving up without a fight.

"No," Liam said flatly.

"What do you mean *no*? Lou already hired me. I flew all the way out here from California." She couldn't stay there. She just couldn't. It would have meant watching another ballerina dance her role in *Cinderella*. It would have meant watching Sasha, the other soloist, get better and better while her foot rotted in a cast.

At least here she'd be doing something worthwhile. Something still related to ballet. She needed this, regardless of the fact that Liam was her boss.

"No." This time the protest was so loud that it roused Liam's massive dog from sleep. He flattened his ears and cocked his giant head. "I never said I needed a ballet teacher. I said I needed help with the girls' after-school program."

Maybe Liam didn't work at the pond anymore, but it was clear that some things around here hadn't changed in the slightest. He was about as far from being a ballet enthusiast as Alaska was from San Francisco.

"Exactly. That's why I'm here." She waited for him to say something. He didn't. He just stared blankly at her. "You mean Lou didn't tell you?"

Liam jammed his hands on his hips. "Tell me what, exactly?"

Good grief. Lou hadn't told him anything? Was she really the one who had to break it to him? Somehow she had the feeling the news would have been better coming from someone else. *Anyone* else.

Super. Just super.

She pasted on a smile. "The new girls' after-school program is ballet."

Liam stared at his reflection, warped and tiny, looking back at him in the shiny gold nameplate on Lou McNeil's desk. It was a perfect representation of how he felt at the moment—warped and tiny. As if he were living in some sort of alternate universe.

Posy was back. And according to her, she worked for him now. Teaching ballet. And how was it that she was calling the senior pastor by his first name? *Lou.* The single syllable had rolled off her tongue as if they were old friends. Liam had worked for the man day in, day out for four years, and he still called him Pastor McNeil.

He was even faintly nervous sitting here in the pastor's office. He told himself he felt like a teenager appearing before the principal only because Posy was sitting beside him. They'd been inseparable back in their school days. For a while, anyway.

He wondered if he should have left Sundog back in the fellowship hall to continue foraging through the garbage. Presently, he was sprawled on the floor with his head resting on Liam's foot. Liam had never thought twice about bringing the dog to work. Half the reason he'd adopted the beast was to give the kids a dog to play with. Funny how none of them had mistaken him for a bear.

"Lou." There it was again. *Lou.* Seated in the chair beside him, Posy aimed a smile across the desk toward Pastor McNeil. "It seems there's been some sort of misunderstanding."

The understatement of the century.

Liam leaned forward in his chair. "Posy says she's here to teach ballet."

"Posy?" Pastor McNeil's face went blank for a moment. "Oh, you mean Miss Sutton. Josephine."

"Josephine?" Liam blinked. Had he gone mad and forgotten everyone's name all of a sudden? Pastor McNeil was now Lou, and Posy had morphed into someone named Josephine?

"That's me." Posy smiled innocently, as if up and changing one's name was an everyday occurrence.

Liam stared at her. "Since when?"

"Since I left Alaska. I guess you could say it's my stage name, and it just sort of stuck." She shrugged, but the implied nonchalance of the gesture was belied by a barely discernible tremor in her hands, knotted in her lap. Nerves. She'd always been good at hiding them.

And Liam had always been good at seeing the parts of her that others missed. Apparently some things, unlike names, never changed.

Did she really expect him to call her Josephine now? He wasn't sure he could do that. It would probably be better for everyone involved if Josephine, whoever she was, danced back to San Francisco.

He directed his attention back to his boss. "*Josephine* says she's here to teach ballet."

The senior pastor's gaze flitted back and forth between the two of them before landing on Liam. "That's right."

Liam shook his head. Maybe if he shook it hard enough,

he could undo whatever was happening. "I don't understand."

"You indicated you needed help with the after-school program, did you not?" Pastor McNeil eyed him over the top of his glasses.

"Yes, I did." *But I said absolutely nothing about ballet.*

Liam's boss shrugged. "You've got the boys busy with the competitive snowballing team, right?"

At the mention of the word *snowball*, Sundog lifted his head, ears pricked forward at attention.

"Competitive snowballing?" Posy slid her gaze toward Liam. "Seriously? That's a thing?"

He lifted a brow. "Yes, it's a thing. An *Alaskan* thing."

"It's like dodgeball, only with snowballs," Pastor McNeil said.

Sundog let out an excited woof. Posy nearly jumped out of her chair.

Likening competitive snowballing to dodgeball was a rather oversimplified explanation, but it would give her a good enough idea. And Liam didn't feel like elaborating at the moment. They weren't here to discuss his snowball project with the boys. They were here to discuss ballet at the church. Or, if Liam had anything to do with it, the absence of ballet.

He attempted to guide the conversation back to the matter at hand. "I'm confused. How did this come about? Posy hasn't set foot in Alaska in seven years."

"Six years. Not seven. Six." At least she hadn't insisted he keep calling her Josephine.

Liam's jaw tensed. He didn't need her to remind him how long it had been. He knew, down to the day—the day they'd graduated. It had been six years and seven months, which was closer to seven years than six.

Pastor McNeil, who'd been quietly observing their bickering, spoke up. "As it seems you two know one another,

Liam, I'm sure you're familiar with the fact that Miss Sutton's mother is a member of our congregation. She read about the job opening in the church bulletin and recommended her daughter for the position."

Posy sat up a little straighter. "It's only temporary. For six weeks. My mother told you that, right?"

Temporary.

Of course it was. Now things were making more sense. She couldn't dance while her foot was in a cast, and she needed something to do. Once her injury was healed, she'd be on the first plane out of here.

But could Liam work with her every day for six weeks? If she'd been healthy, probably. The fact that she was injured complicated things. In a major way. He wasn't sure he could go through that again. And he knew for a fact he couldn't watch her go through it. Not if the past repeated itself.

"Yes, I understand." Pastor McNeil nodded at Posy. "But a temporary program is better than no program at all."

Liam decided to cut to the chase. They were talking in circles. "I'm just not sure ballet is the answer."

In fact, he was sure it was *not* the answer. So sure that he'd just about decided to form two competitive snowball teams. The girls could pelt one another with snowballs just as easily as the boys could.

Except the girls had made it pretty clear they weren't interested in snowballing. If only Ronnie Goodwin hadn't hit Melody Tucker in the head with a particularly wet snowball on the first day of practice. Maybe Liam could get the girls helmets.

Right. As if the church could afford such luxuries. There was a reason he'd chosen snowballing as a team sport for the boys. If there was one thing Alaska had in abundance, it was snow. Free for the taking.

What he needed to do most of all was get a handle on the apparent feud between Ronnie and Melody. The two teens couldn't stand one another. Lately, their disagreements had begun to spill over and affect the rest of the kids in youth group. And that was a problem—a problem he could deal with, however, unlike ballet. Ballet was an enemy he no longer had the will to fight. He'd been on the losing end of that battle too many times before.

"There's nothing wrong with ballet," Posy said quietly. But she didn't meet his gaze.

There was plenty wrong with ballet. Was she really going to make him rehash everything, right here in front of his boss?

No. He couldn't go there. Something about it felt wrong. "Forgive me for pointing out the obvious, but you're on crutches. How are you going to teach dance?"

If his words wounded her, she gave no indication. She smiled sweetly at Lou and ignored Liam altogether. "My foot won't be a problem. The girls are beginners, right? Demonstrating the most basic steps won't be a strain. Besides, I'll be off the crutches and in a soft walking cast in no time."

Pastor McNeil—*Lou*—smiled, as if a dance teacher with a five-pound weight attached to her foot and a pair of wobbly crutches was the most ordinary thing in the world. Were they that desperate for help in the youth department?

Yes. Yes, they were. The job posting had been circulating for months. Posy was the only remotely qualified applicant in all that time.

"That sounds promising, Miss Sutton. Certainly promising enough to give it a try." Lou aimed a pointed glance at Liam. "Wouldn't you agree?"

Liam didn't agree. Not at all. But he was running out of objections he was willing to discuss. And Lou was already looking at him as if he were borderline nuts.

"Liam, you'll work with the boys. Miss Sutton will work with the girls. I fail to see how this is a problem. Unless there's something you're not telling me?"

Now was the time to speak up. But what could he possibly say that wouldn't make him sound like a lovesick teenager?

I loved her. But she loved ballet more, even though it took everything from her.

He glanced at Posy for the briefest of moments, and in her eyes he saw all the words he couldn't bring himself to say. She'd walked away from him so easily back then that he'd sometimes wondered if she ever fully understood what had happened. Did she not see how badly she'd hurt herself, and in doing so, how badly she'd hurt him? He would have walked through fire for the girl she'd been. What they'd ended up walking through together had been far worse.

Looking at her now, he could see those moments shining back at him in her eyes. She hadn't forgotten after all.

He aimed his gaze back at his boss. "No, nothing."

"All right, then." Pastor McNeil stood, a sure sign the discussion was over. "Tomorrow afternoon, the fellowship hall will become Miss Sutton's ballet studio."

A ballet studio. Liam's head was on the verge of exploding.

What have I done?

Chapter Three

Whoever invented circular revolving doors had obviously never been on crutches.

Posy felt like a newborn moose wobbling around on unfamiliar, gangly legs as she spun her way inside the Northern Lights Inn. Then, just as the instrument of torture spilled her out, the tip of her left crutch got stuck between one of the glass panels of the door and its frame. She jerked on the crutch as hard as she could, but it didn't budge. The revolving door ceased revolving altogether, trapping two men wearing fur-trimmed parkas and unhappy scowls inside.

Pilots, in all likelihood. The Northern Lights Inn overlooked a lake that remained frozen for at least nine months out of the year and served as the local municipal airport. Snow planes took off and landed on skis, making regular runs into Anchorage for supplies, or out into the Bush—the parts of Alaska inaccessible by roads, which was the overwhelming majority of the state. At all hours of the day and night, the hotel's coffee bar was a gathering place for local charter pilots, along with the severely under-caffeinated looking for relief.

Now that Posy got a better look at the two men she'd

trapped in the revolving door, she suspected they fell into the latter category. They looked as though they could each use a cup of coffee. Or three.

Sorry she mouthed at them from the other side of the glass, yanking again on the crutch. All at once it came dislodged, and Posy nearly fell on her backside for the second time in less than an hour. So much for balletic grace and poise.

One of the two men helped her get resituated on her crutches before making a beeline for the coffee bar.

Posy paused for a second before heading that direction herself. She hated this. Absolutely hated not having perfect control over her movements. Ballet was all about control. When she lifted her leg in an attitude position, her knee raised at the exact same angle every time. That was what all those hours of barre work and practice were for—making sure every pointed toe, every classically arched arm and every graceful step were absolutely perfect. She felt out of sorts, as if she were walking around in a strange body.

She looked around the dark wood-paneled walls of the Northern Lights Inn and the sweeping views of the Chugach Mountain Range afforded by the coffee bar's big picture window, expecting at least a tiny wave of nostalgia to wash over her. It didn't. Being back in Alaska was even stranger than she'd expected. It no longer felt like home.

Strange body. Strange town.

Somewhere in her head she heard Liam's voice again.

You've been gone a long time.

Her throat grew tight for some odd reason, and she suddenly felt like crying. Which was patently ridiculous. So she had a broken bone in her foot. It would heal. In a matter of six weeks it would heal, and she'd be back in San Francisco doing what she loved most: dancing. Her foot would repair itself, good as new. Just as it had before.

It had to.

Everything was going to be fine. She was rattled, that was all. It might be home, but Alaska was the polar opposite of San Francisco. A sea change. And she'd had her feet on the snowy ground for only two hours. Anyone would be disoriented. What she needed right now was coffee. And her girlfriends.

"Posy! You're really here. I can't believe it." Zoey Wynne, her oldest childhood friend, hopped off one of the bar stools at the coffee bar and wrapped her in a tight embrace.

"I'm here, all right." Posy kept a grip on her wayward crutches and let herself be hugged.

The moment Zoey let her go, Posy found herself in the arms of Anya Parker, another close friend from the days of skating at the pond and trekking through the woods on snowshoes after school. It was nice being hugged. Dancers hugged one another all the time on performance nights— good-luck hugs in the dressing rooms, congratulatory hugs in the wings. But it had been a while since she'd been embraced like this.

Like it mattered.

Posy's soul breathed a relieved sigh. For the first time since she'd been back, Aurora, Alaska, actually felt like home.

"Come sit down." Anya glanced briefly at the cast on Posy's foot, but if she was shocked to see it, she didn't let it show.

News traveled fast. For once, Posy was grateful for small-town gossip. She'd spent enough time dwelling on her injury without having to explain it again and again.

She slid onto one of the bar stools and ordered a cup of coffee. Black, with the smallest possible amount of sugar.

"Gosh, this is good." She closed her eyes, savoring the first sip. "I'd forgotten how great the coffee is here."

Anya snickered. "Don't they have coffee in San Francisco?"

"Theater coffee." Posy shook her head, thinking about the food truck perpetually parked at the curb by the back door of the theater where her company rehearsed six days a week. She shuddered to think about how many to-go cups of coffee she'd consumed from that truck over the course of the past six years. "Not the same thing at all."

"It's all part of our plan." Zoey winked at Anya and then aimed her gaze back at Posy. "We've got you here, finally. Now we're going to convince you to stay by pouring Alaska's finest java down your throat."

Posy gave her an uneasy smile. She had no intention of staying once her foot was healed. What in the world would she do in Aurora? Work for Liam the rest of her life?

Anya frowned. "What was that look for?"

"What look?" Posy shrugged and drained the remainder of her coffee.

"That look on your face just now. The one that indicated staying here would be a fate worse than death." Zoey's eyebrows lifted.

Half a dozen years had passed, and her friends could still read her like a book. "It's not like that. I'm happy to be back. If I can't dance, there's no place I'd rather be."

She wiggled her toes in her cast just the slightest bit. Pain shot from her foot all the way up her shin.

Please, God. Please let me be able to dance again.

"Then what's wrong? Because you seem less than thrilled." Anya covered Posy's hand with her own. "Are you worried about your foot? It's the same one, isn't it?"

Yes, it was the same one. And yes, she was worried. But Posy didn't think that was what Anya really wanted to know. "I'm taking care of it. I promise."

"You're not still dancing, are you?" Zoey asked.

"No." She laughed and motioned toward the cast. "It's a little difficult with this ball and chain."

Unlike last time, there was no hiding the fact that she

was injured. The cast guaranteed that much, as had her spectacular fall in the middle of *Cinderella*. She was walking around with her heart visible for the entire world to see.

The other time had been different. The break hadn't occurred with the drama of a sickening crack, but over time. A stress fracture. At first, Posy had thought she'd just been overdoing it. It was audition season. High school graduation was right around the corner. She'd been traveling on weekends, trying out for spots in various dance companies up and down the West Coast. Of course, her dream was to dance in Seattle or even Anchorage. Somewhere close to home. Close to Liam.

She'd felt so torn between the two of them—Liam and ballet. She'd loved dance for as long as she could remember. Her parents told stories of how she'd bounced to the beat of push-button toys in the church nursery when she was only two years old.

Somewhere deep down she possessed an unquenchable need to move in the presence of music. She didn't just hear music. She felt it, down to her core. And her ability to move to it, to dance, was God-given. She'd known that since before she could fully articulate it.

Then Liam had come along. And for the first time, she'd felt the same way about a person that she'd felt about ballet. It was bewildering. It was exhilarating. It was love. But they were young. And why should she have to choose? Being a dancer didn't mean she couldn't be in love.

After two weeks of icing her throbbing foot at night under the covers of her bed so her parents wouldn't see, Posy had known something was seriously wrong. She couldn't walk without limping. And when she danced, she had to bite the inside of her lip to keep from crying out in pain. She should have told someone then. She didn't. She didn't breathe a word about it to anyone, not even Liam.

She should have said something. She should have gone

straight to the doctor instead of doing her best to wish it away as she danced on, from one audition to the next, for fear of missing out on her big chance at becoming a professional ballerina.

She should have done a lot of things differently.

"I'm not taking any pills, if that's what you're wondering. Not even Advil," Posy said.

It was humiliating to have to give these kinds of assurances. Humiliating, but necessary. She might as well get used to it. Anya and Zoey had both been wondering. She could see it on their faces, just as she'd seen it in Liam's eyes as they'd sat next to one another in the pastor's office.

"Good." Anya gave her hand a squeeze before letting go.

"Seriously. It's not the foot that's bothering me so much as something else." Or *someone* else.

Zoey frowned. "What's wrong, then?"

Posy looked up, and her gazed fixed on the stuffed grizzly bear that stood in the corner behind the coffee bar. Like she needed an enormous furry reminder of the stellar afternoon she'd had. "Liam Blake. That's what's wrong. Liam and his gigantic dog."

Anya's eyebrows rose. "You've already seen Liam?"

"Not only have I seen him, but I'm apparently working for him. He's my boss." Posy stared into her empty coffee cup, willing it to refill itself. She was going to need more caffeine to process the specifics of her new life, however temporary. Massive amounts of caffeine.

Anya asked the barista for refills all around.

Zoey shook her head. "Wait. Are you working at the church now, or…?"

"The church, yes." Posy sighed. It was difficult to fathom that only two hours ago, she'd been so excited about the prospect of teaching ballet that she'd headed straight to the church once her plane had landed. The fact that the route from the airport to church allowed her to avoid Aurora's town square and the big evergreen tree that stood at its center was merely convenient. "I'm teaching ballet in the after-school program."

Anya choked on her coffee. "Ballet? At the church? Does Liam know?"

Posy nodded. "He does now. And needless to say, he's less than thrilled."

Even after she'd gotten over the initial shock of realizing that Liam was the youth pastor, she'd thought that maybe, just maybe, his feelings about ballet had changed. A lot of time had passed. She'd hoped it would have been enough time for him to realize it wasn't ballet that had hurt her. Dancing might have been the cause of her stress fracture, but dancing hadn't made her hide her injury. Ballet hadn't shoved those pills down her throat. She'd done those things herself.

She'd been afraid. Afraid of losing her chance at becoming a ballerina. Afraid to find out just what was wrong with her body. God had created her to be a ballet dancer. If she could no longer dance, she no longer knew who she was.

And that had been the irony of the whole ordeal, hadn't it? She'd never questioned the fact that God had given her the ability to dance, but once the pain came, she'd lost her faith. It had left her so swiftly, she'd never realized it was gone.

The mess had been one of her own making.

"I didn't even know Liam worked there." Posy added another dash of sugar to her fresh cup of coffee. "How long has he been the youth pastor, anyway?"

Anya and Zoey grew very quiet. Finally, Anya answered the question.

"A long time. Four years," she said.

Four years? Liam had been a pastor for four years, and

she hadn't heard a thing about it? How was that possible? "You're kidding."

Anya shook her head. "No, I'm not kidding. I'm dead serious. Lou McNeil came to Aurora from Anchorage to take over as the head pastor, and he hired Liam straightaway. It seems Pastor McNeil knows Liam's dad."

"So Liam's dad is still preaching?" Posy asked.

"Yes, although I have no idea where." Anya reached for the half-and-half and added a dollop to her coffee. "No one can keep up with Liam's parents. Once they sold their house here, they stopped coming back to Aurora altogether. Not that they ever spent much time here to begin with."

So the house had sold.

Posy's last memory of Liam's childhood home had been the day his dad had driven the post of the for-sale sign into the nearly frozen yard. A stake through Liam's heart.

"You mean your mom never told you that Liam is a pastor now?" Zoey asked.

"No. She didn't." Posy set down her coffee cup. Suddenly, she was no longer thirsty.

Surely her mom didn't want her to work at the church so Liam could keep an eye on her. That couldn't be possible. Her parents couldn't actually expect her old boyfriend to make sure she handled her injury better than she had last time. Because that would be mortifying beyond words. And wrong. Just plain wrong.

"You know, all of this awkwardness could have been avoided if you'd come back to visit. Even once," Zoey said, her tone not at all judgmental, but wistful.

Anya nodded, her gaze flitting ever so briefly to the sparkling diamond on her ring finger. She was married now. As was Zoey. And Posy hadn't even met their husbands.

"You know I have my pilot's license now, right? And

my own plane?" Zoey's face lit up the way Posy's always did when she slipped on a pristine pair of pointe shoes.

"Now, that I did know." Her mother had filled her in on that much. Funny how she'd remembered to mention Zoey's plane, but not the fact that Posy would be working with Liam. She and her mom were going to have a chat about that. Soon. Very soon. "Actually, I wanted to ask you if you could fly me to Anchorage a few times a week for my physical-therapy appointments for my foot."

Zoey grinned. "Of course. I'd love that. We can fly over the ranch, and you can see the reindeer. They look so pretty from the sky."

Posy had almost forgotten. Zoey and her husband lived on a reindeer farm.

She'd missed so much.

Liam was a man of God now, Zoey was both a pilot and a reindeer farmer, and Posy wasn't the only one with a different name. Anya and Zoey both had new last names. Her mother had told her all about their weddings, of course, but seeing the shiny rings on their fingers made it seem much more real than it had from far away.

They were her closest friends. Granted, she hadn't seen them in a while, and she definitely could have been better about keeping in touch. But they still knew more about her than any of her San Francisco friends. They cared. They genuinely cared. And they were married to men Posy had never laid eyes on. Perfect strangers.

"Don't worry." Anya gave her a friendly nudge. "We'll get you all caught up on everything you've missed. Before long, you'll know more than you ever wanted to know about the fair citizens of Aurora. Right, Zoey?"

"Oh, sure. Where to start… Let's see. Did you know that Anya's husband sometimes dresses up as a bear?"

Just what Posy needed. Another bear scare. "What?"

Anya rolled her eyes. "It's not as silly as it sounds. Trust me."

The two of them launched into a laughter-filled discussion about everyone in Aurora—people Posy knew and others she'd never heard of before. She managed to keep up with the conversation, making mental notes every now and then of new names. There were new babies, new marriages, new stores, new streets. Even new dogs, Liam's shaggy beast included.

But as Posy sat with her two oldest friends, drinking coffee and chatting like old times, she was beginning to get the feeling that the only stranger in town was one named Josephine.

"Stay here." Liam aimed a stern look toward the passenger sitting beside him in the front seat of his Jeep. "And try to resist the urge to eat anything. The headrest, for instance."

Oblivious, Sundog panted, his tongue hanging sideways out of his mouth.

Liam issued one final warning before exiting the vehicle. "I'm being serious. Stay. Behave. Or whatever the proper command is for this situation."

He was probably going to have to do something about the plundering problem. And the chewing. Posy hadn't been altogether wrong when she'd called the dog unruly. But Liam liked to give him the benefit of the doubt. He was a rescue. He'd lived on the streets. It was only normal for him to worry about where the next meal was coming from. Liam just wished it wasn't the stuffing of the Jeep's passenger seat, as it had been last time. Or the center of the bedroom mattress back at his house.

Yep. He probably needed to take a training class or something, but with the sudden reappearance of Posy, Sundog had shifted to a lower position on the priority list. Oh, how he longed for the time when chewed-up pillows were his biggest problem.

Was it only this morning that she'd shown up at the church?

He felt as though he'd lived a lifetime since then, and it wasn't even dark outside yet.

He glanced at his watch. Half an hour until school got out. He needed to make this quick so he could get back to the church in time. He never left the premises this late in the day, but he'd heard Posy telling Lou that she was getting together with Anya and Zoey at the Northern Lights Inn this afternoon. Now might be his only chance. He would already be working with her day in and day out. He definitely didn't want her finding him standing in the living room of her childhood home.

He rang the doorbell and waited, shooting a final glance at Sundog, who already appeared to be gnawing on the dashboard.

The door swung open, and Posy's mother stood on the other side of the threshold. Just like old times. Really old times. "Liam. What a surprise."

"Mrs. Sutton." He nodded. "May I come in?"

"Of course, of course. Please do." She held the door open wide, and Liam stepped into the past.

Everything was the same, at least everything within Liam's field of vision. Same gold-framed mirror hanging in the entryway—the one where Posy had always checked her reflection right before she breezed out the door for school, ballet class or a day at the pond. Same brown leather sofa where he'd sat on more than one occasion with a boxed corsage in his hands, waiting for her to come downstairs so he could take her to the school dance. He resisted the urge to look at those stairs now, half-afraid that same tingle-tangle of anticipation would stir in his gut.

As though she were about to descend that staircase wearing a pretty tulle dress and a smile just for him.

He cleared his throat and tried to shake the memories, breathing a sigh of relief when he spotted the new big-screen television hanging above the fireplace mantel, a shiny, hi-def reminder that he hadn't, in fact, stepped inside a time warp.

"Can I get you anything, Liam?" Mrs. Sutton gestured toward the kitchen, where Liam knew a pitcher of Alaskan blackberry tea rested on the top shelf of the refrigerator and a ceramic cookie jar shaped like a black bear cub sat atop the butcher-block counter.

This was just a little too surreal for his taste. Better to get in and out. Besides, the kids would be arriving at the church soon. "No, thank you."

"Have a seat, then. Make yourself at home." She gestured toward the sofa.

Make yourself at home.

Liam purposefully sank into one of the upholstered armchairs with his back to the staircase. "I'm sorry to drop by unannounced like this."

"It's no trouble at all, Liam. You're always welcome here." She offered him a motherly smile.

Mrs. Sutton had always been fond of him, even before that night he'd shown up at this very house, rain-soaked, heart torn in two as he spilled each and every one of Posy's secrets. Afterward, Posy's parents had put him on a virtual pedestal. So high up he was out of Posy's reach.

He swallowed. He didn't like to think about that night. And he hadn't. For the better part of six and a half years, he'd managed to successfully put it out of his head. But along with Posy, all those memories had come rushing back this afternoon.

"How are your parents, Liam?"

"Great, I suppose." He hadn't actually spoken to them

in weeks. A month maybe. But their latest postcard had arrived the other day. From Kivalina, 125 miles north of the Arctic Circle, which made it one of Alaska's most remote villages.

"Do they have any plans to visit soon?" Mrs. Sutton smiled warmly. She'd never really understood his parents.

Liam wasn't altogether sure he understood them himself. As overinvolved as the Suttons could be in their daughter's life, his parents swung in the opposite direction. They were more interested in seeing every square inch of frozen tundra this side of the North Pole than they were in the particulars of Liam's life. They didn't know about the dog. Or the new lights he'd strung across the skating pond. Or that he'd stopped dating Sara, and that breakup had occurred over four months ago. Not that he thought of it as an actual breakup. They'd gone out once or twice a week for a few months, but that special spark had never been there. It had been casual. All of Liam's relationships had been casual since Posy.

He cleared his throat. "My folks don't have any plans to visit, so far as I know. Getting planes in and out of the Arctic Circle can be complicated."

"I'm sure it is. Give them our regards the next time you talk to them, okay?"

Liam nodded, not wanting to make any outright promises. Conversations full of static from his dad's satellite phone didn't leave much room for small talk. Besides, he wasn't here to talk about his parents.

"Posy's back," he said, his voice sounding altogether too raw and vulnerable for his liking.

"Yes, she is." Mrs. Sutton nodded. "We haven't seen her yet, but she should be home in time for dinner."

"She's staying here?" he asked. A dumb question. Where else would she be staying? Why was his brain suddenly on vacation?

"Yes."

"Good." His smile felt strained. He was just going to have to bite the bullet and say what he'd come here to say before he ran out of time. Or lost his nerve. "Look, I know you told her about the job at the church."

Mrs. Sutton's gaze suddenly shifted to the floor.

"I also know that you didn't tell her I worked there," he said quietly.

"I wasn't sure she'd take the job if she knew, and it's the perfect place for her to be while she gets better."

They were getting to the crux of the matter. Finally. "Why is that?"

Nervous laughter spilled from Mrs. Sutton's mouth. "Working at the church will be good for her. She'll be surrounded by the love of God and the girls…"

Liam leveled his gaze at her. "And me."

Her only response was a quiet sigh, followed by uncomfortable silence.

"I can't do it, Mrs. Sutton. I just can't." His throat burned all of a sudden. Seared with memories of words that he would not, could not, utter again. "I can't be the one to keep an eye on her. That's what you want, isn't it? That's why you sent her to the church, and that's why you didn't tell her I'd be there."

He waited for her to admit it, not that he really needed confirmation of his suspicions. Everything about Posy's return was a little too coincidental to be believable.

"You're right." Posy's mother gave a slow, reluctant nod. "I'm sorry. I should have spoken to you about it first. I'm worried about her, Liam. So is her father. Did she tell you about her injury?"

Guilt hovered around the edges of Liam's consciousness. Posy hadn't told him a thing because he hadn't asked. "No."

"It's a fracture." Mrs. Sutton gulped. Her eyes grew

shiny with the threat of unshed tears. "Her fifth metatarsal."

Fifth metatarsal.

Despite the fact that Posy's health was no longer any of his concern, Liam felt those two words like a blow to his chest. In medical circles, a fracture of the fifth metatarsal was sometimes called the Dancer's Fracture. Liam didn't run in medical circles, but he knew plenty about such an injury.

"So it's the same injury as last time," he said.

"Worse, I'm afraid. She broke it all at once, in the middle of a performance."

Morbid images of Posy falling to the ground in an agonizing twisted cloud of tulle and sequins flooded Liam's imagination. He squeezed his eyes closed until they faded. "She told Pastor McNeil her foot would heal in six weeks, then she was returning to the ballet company."

"That's what she says. She's up for a promotion, and if she can't dance in six weeks she'll lose her chance." Mrs. Sutton had begun wringing her hands.

Liam's headache made a swift return. So Posy's body had a deadline hanging over it? Six weeks to heal or else? Perfect. Just perfect.

He dropped his head in his hands.

Why, God? I don't want this. I don't.

Posy's mom spoke again, dragging him back to the present. "I'm not asking you to save her from herself. I know that would be expecting too much, especially after all this time. But you've always known Posy better than anyone else does. You see her. She can't hide from you like she can from the rest of us. She never could. Can't you just watch her? Simply be there and let us know if something seems wrong?"

She made it sound so easy, so simple. No more complicated than making sure a child stayed out of harm's way.

Don't play in the street. Don't talk to strangers. Don't run with scissors.

But Posy wasn't a child. She was a grown woman. A grown woman with a new name and a new life. A new life that didn't include Liam. How could he sit here across from Posy's mother and tell her that what she was asking was impossible? Even if he wanted to take on such a role—which he most definitely did not—it would have been utterly impossible.

He might have known her once upon a time. But things were different. She wasn't his girl anymore. He wasn't sure she ever had been.

Chapter Four

A few hours after leaving Posy's house, Liam stood at the edge of the pond—*his* pond, a concept he still sometimes found difficult to believe—and watched Ronnie walk gingerly across the frozen surface carrying a bucket of warm water. Sundog sat at Liam's feet, tail wagging, ears alert, and on Liam's other side, his friend Alec Wynne stood shaking his head.

"That kid is going to fall on his backside," Alec said.

Liam frowned. "Not if he's careful."

He didn't want Ronnie to get hurt. Of course he didn't, even though the boy had been driving him a little nuts lately.

"Now what do I do?" Ronnie asked, staring down at the ice at his feet.

"Look for the chipped spots and pour some water over them." Liam pointed to the far right end of the pond where Melody did most of her jumps when she came by to practice, which was becoming a more and more frequent occurrence. "They tend to accumulate over there, mostly."

"Got it, Pastor." Ronnie tightened his grip on the bucket and started slipping and sliding in that direction.

Alec shook his head again. "Are you paying him, or is this slave labor?"

"I'm paying him. A little." Liam picked up the hose and filled another bucket. Sundog bit at the stream of water, as if he could catch it in his massive jaws. "It's also a penance of sorts."

Alec laughed. "For?"

"For intentionally throwing a snowball at Melody Tucker's face."

"Ouch." Alec winced.

"Yeah. This thing between him and Melody is becoming a problem." Thus far, Liam's only strategy for solving the problem involved chores. Fortunately, there was no shortage of chores that needed to be done at the pond.

Alec crossed his arms. "Let me guess. Young love?"

Liam forgot what he was doing for a moment, and water sloshed over the edge of his last bucket. He threw the hose down and turned off the spigot. "Young love? I sure hope not." He hoped not with every fiber of his being.

Alec's eyebrows rose. "Constant bickering? Unmerciful teasing? One minute he's nice to her, and the next minute he's throwing snow in her face?"

That sounded uncomfortably accurate. "Pretty much, yeah."

"It's love. Trust me."

Great. The last item Liam needed on his substantial to-do list was dealing with two lovesick teenagers. Especially now.

"Speaking of young love…" Alec gave him a sideways glance.

Liam held up a hand and sighed. "Don't start. Please."

He'd thought, *hoped*, he could avoid talking about Posy. At least with Alec. Alec was a transplant. He'd been in Aurora for only six months or so. But he was also married to one of Posy's best friends, so the notion that he'd have no idea about Liam and Posy's tumultuous history had undoubtedly been a pipe dream from the start.

"So long as you're handling it well. And clearly you are." Alec shot him a wry smile.

Liam handed him a bucket. "Here. And yes, *you* are most definitely slave labor."

Alec laughed, and crunched through the tightly packed snow and onto the surface of the pond. The fine layer of ice atop the snow was due to the unseasonably cold drop in temperature the night before, as were the chips on the surface of the ice. In severely cold weather, ice grew brittle. Brittle ice chipped.

Liam knew that much now. His learning curve since he'd purchased the skating pond had been a big one. He'd taken the plunge as simply a moneymaking venture. Youth pastors weren't exactly overpaid, and the pond was a key component in Aurora's nightlife. Its *only* component, for all practical purposes. When the for-sale sign had gone up, Liam had cashed in the college fund he'd never used and become a skating-rink owner.

But it had quickly become a labor of love. He'd always had an attachment to the pond, like most everything about Aurora. About Aurora itself.

When he'd landed here as a teen, he'd had enough of the nomadic lifestyle that came with being a circuit preacher's kid. Enough of moving from one village to the next, each one somehow seemingly more and more remote. Enough of being a guest in other people's homes instead of sleeping in a bed of his own.

And enough of planes. Planes, planes and more planes. The smell of airplane fuel still made him feel a little sick inside.

He'd wanted a home. A town. A place that was his.

He'd told his parents as much the day they'd unpacked their bags in Aurora. He was staying put. He wanted to make friends, go to a regular school, try out for the base-ball team...do all the things normal kids did. He'd seen virtually nothing of the town yet. Just the tree...that fate-ful tree. Stretching its beautiful blue, snow-laden boughs over everything. Welcoming arms.

His mom and dad had prayed about his announcement, discussed it for days on end. Finally, they'd agreed to buy a house and stay put for three years. Just until he gradu-ated from high school. His dad would come and go as his job required, but Liam, his mother and his brother would stay right there in Aurora.

Liam had been elated. He'd thrown himself into life in Aurora. He'd loved that town. And it had loved him right back. And in time, Aurora—its people, its icicle air, its permafrost ground—had become home.

And now he owned a piece of that town. A piece of its heart. At times, he couldn't believe it. Then something would happen. The temperature would drop suddenly, and the surface of the ice would crack. Or they'd get an unexpected heavy rain, a layer of shale ice would cover the pond, and he'd have to scrape the entire surface. Un-doubtedly, Liam would be reminded that he was indeed the owner and operator of an outdoor skating rink.

"No more chips. Everything looks good." Alec stepped off the ice and tossed the empty bucket into the snow.

Liam wound the hose and turned the water faucet until it was just shy of the off position. A fraction of an inch could make the difference between being stuck with fro-zen pipes and maintaining his sanity. "Thanks, man. I appreciate the help. There's never a shortage of things to do around here."

"No problem." Alec grinned in Ronnie's direction. "With any luck, your boy over there will keep getting in trouble, and you'll have so much help you won't know what to do with all of your free time."

Sundog flopped on his back and shimmied in the snow, sending a wave of powder flying ten feet. In two seconds flat, Liam was buried up to his shins. "Bored? Doubtful."

"Pastor? *Pastor!*" Ronnie called from midway across the ice. He skidded toward the edge while juggling his empty red bucket.

"Don't look now, but that trouble I mentioned is about to rear its ugly head," Alec muttered under his breath.

The crunch of tires on snow caused Liam to turn around, and when he saw the familiar silver truck, he knew at once why Ronnie was in such a hurry to get off the ice.

He turned back around, and sure enough, Ronnie stood before him, red-faced from exertion, scowling at Melody's truck. "What's *she* doing here?"

Liam inhaled calmly. "Melody practices here sometimes before the pond opens up for the night. You know that."

Ronnie rolled his eyes. "She thinks she's going to be a real skater one day. Please."

"She already is a real skater." Graceful. Almost balletic. Sometimes it was like watching a memory glide over the frosted mirror surface of the ice. "Why don't you stick around while she skates? I think you'll be impressed."

Ronnie looked at Liam in abject horror. "No. Way."

Behind his back, Alec stifled a grin.

"Ronnie." Liam lifted a brow. A warning.

"I mean no, thanks." Ronnie shoved his hands in his pockets and looked everywhere except in the direction of the truck, where Melody was climbing down from the passenger seat, her skates slung over her shoulder by their laces. "I've got homework."

Sure he did.

"All right. I'll see you tomorrow after school, then," Liam said.

"See you, Pastor." Ronnie trudged toward his rust bucket of a car.

Liam called after him, "Thanks for the help fixing the ice."

Ronnie waved, steadfastly avoiding Melody's gaze as she walked past him. Once he'd just about reached his car, he turned slightly. He ventured a glance at Melody right as she looked at him over her shoulder. She smiled. He smiled in return, then seemed to realize what he was doing. He scowled. She scowled back and stomped toward a bench to sit and put on her skates.

"What did I tell you?" Alec muttered. "Young love. It's a classic case."

Liam's gut tightened. Alec was right. How had he not seen it before? The two of them were about as subtle as a moose in striped pajamas.

Then again, what had Liam ever known about love?

Posy had never felt so exhausted and yet so awake at the same time. Three hours and four cups of coffee after arriving at the Northern Lights Inn, she finally left and headed to her parents' house.

Her house. At least she still thought of it as her house, even though she hadn't darkened its door in seven years.

Six. Not seven.

She wanted to strangle Liam. She kept thinking about him sitting beside her, across from Lou, making his case for why she shouldn't be teaching ballet at the church.

I'm just not sure ballet is the answer. Posy hasn't set foot in Alaska in seven years.

It wasn't a crime. People were allowed to leave home. It was normal. Natural. Liam just felt differently about it because of the way he'd been brought up, always moving from place to place. Home was a sacred concept to Liam. Aurora was sacred.

The town was sacred to her, too. Didn't he understand that?

How could he possibly when you left and never looked back?

She slid her key into the lock on the front door, but it was unnecessary. The knob turned and the door fell open, just as it always had. There were no such things as locked doors in Aurora. Just one of the many differences between a tiny Alaskan town and a big city like San Francisco.

She pocketed her key ring and stepped over the threshold. The interior of the house was dark, and she breathed a sigh of relief. She'd intentionally stayed out later than originally planned. After everything that had transpired at the church, she just wasn't up to seeing her parents. Not yet.

"Posy?" a voice called from the darkened living room. "Is that you?"

So much for avoidance.

"Yes, it's me, Mom." She limped into the living room, dragging her rolling suitcase behind her. The television, a huge flat-screen Posy had never seen before, flickered quietly in the dark. "What are you doing awake this time of night?"

Her parents went to bed after the ten o'clock news every night. They watched the weather report, kept up with what was happening in Anchorage and headed to bed right after her dad's favorite feature—the daily moose-sighting report, wherein viewers submitted photos of moose out and about town. Her dad held the record in Aurora for the most moose photos ever shown on the local news. Posy had sent him a new smartphone with a good-quality camera feature to replace his ancient flip phone for his birthday after she'd had her first three months' pay as a professional dancer under her belt. He'd been ecstatic.

"What am I doing awake?" Her mother crossed the living room and gave her a tight hug. For some reason, it felt less comforting than the embraces of her girlfriends. More suffocating. "Waiting for you, of course. Your father headed to bed a little before ten, though. He has an early day tomorrow."

"How early? He went to bed before the moose report?"

"Oh, honey. They don't do the moose report anymore. They haven't for a few years now." Her mother released her. She smiled, and even in the dim light of the silent television, Posy could see lines around her eyes that hadn't been there before.

"Oh. Wow. I had no idea." The demise of the moose report struck her as profoundly sad, which was silly, really.

She probably just needed sleep. She'd had an early-morning four-hour flight to Anchorage, followed by her commuter flight to Aurora. Then the church, followed by the coffee date. It was a tribute to the power of Alaska's finest caffeine that she could still hold her head up.

"People were getting carried away. They decided it was dangerous when Ed Candy from the dry cleaners got trampled and broke his foot while he was chasing a moose into the hospital with a camera."

The hospital? Trampled?

First Liam's crazy dog, now the moose. The animals had gone crazy since she'd been away. Although she could sympathize with poor Ed Candy's broken foot.

Posy's foot throbbed with pain. She'd probably been up and about too much today. She needed to lie down and get it elevated. She needed an ice pack. She needed an Advil. Desperately.

Don't go there.

As if she were reading her mind, Posy's mother asked, "Can I get you anything?"

"Mom, you don't have to wait on me. This is my home, too." Posy forced herself to smile, even though she suddenly felt like crying.

She would not cry. Not now. She shouldn't feel sad. She should feel mad.

She pretended she was onstage and rearranged her features in a mask of neutrality. "I need to talk to you about something."

"Oh?" Her mom's gaze flitted about the room, which told Posy she knew perfectly well what was coming. "It's awfully late. You said so yourself. We can talk in the morning." She extended a hand toward Posy's suitcase.

Posy wheeled it out of reach. "No. I want to talk about it now."

"Okay. Sit down, sit down." Her mom patted the sofa cushions and then took a seat opposite in the chair where her dad used to sit when he watched the moose report. Who knew where he sat these days?

Posy obediently sat sideways on the sofa and propped her foot up on a throw pillow. She wondered how long it was going to take before one of them finally mentioned her injury. "Mom, I appreciate your talking to Lou and getting things in order for me to work at the church, but…"

Tears stung the backs of her eyes again. Why was this so hard to say? She had every right to be upset. But sitting across from her mother, looking at her face—at the new lines around her eyes and the worry in her gaze—her indignation began to slip away.

She should have visited more. She hadn't even come home for Christmas. Not that she ever would have been able to take leave of the ballet company during the holidays. The weeks that stretched from the end of October to New Year's Day made up *Nutcracker* season. Everyone knew as much.

"I wish you would have told me that Liam was the youth pastor," she finally said.

Her mom sighed. "I'm sorry. I just thought…"

"You thought you could have him spy on me. To make

sure I'm not taking any pills. Right?" Her throat burned. It hurt to say the words aloud, but someone had to.

"Posy." The lines around her mother's face deepened.

"Mom, admit it. Please."

Her mom took a deep breath, and she seemed to wilt a little on the exhalation. "That's part of it, yes. But try to understand. Other than the handful of times we've been to California to watch you dance, your father and I haven't seen you in seven years."

"Six," Posy began to whisper, but the word died on her tongue.

"After what happened last time, we wanted you here. At home, where you belong."

Is this where I belong, God?

She didn't bother waiting for an answer.

This was her home, but no, it wasn't where she belonged. Not really. She was just here because she was hurt. She belonged onstage. Her foot belonged in a ballet shoe, not the ugly plaster where it currently resided.

"It's not like the last time, Mom. I promise."

Her mother nodded. She didn't believe her. She might want to, but she didn't. That much was obvious. And Posy wasn't altogether sure she blamed her.

God, why is this all so hard?

Posy glanced up at the ceiling. But instead of finding God, all she could imagine were the snow-laden boughs of the giant blue evergreen spread over the town like angels' wings.

Chapter Five

The next afternoon at the church, Posy scrolled through the playlists on her iPod, checking one last time to make sure she had the music she needed for barre work. Classical, of course.

For as long as she could remember, her barre exercises had been performed to classical piano. Sharp, staccato notes, perfect for the seemingly endless repetition of pliés, elevés, tendus and battements.

When she'd been a little girl in Madame Sylvie's ballet school, the one and only in Aurora, the music had drifted from an ancient turntable—blue, the kind that could be closed like a suitcase. On it spun scratchy vinyl record albums with cardboard covers on the verge of deterioration that had been used by generations of dancers.

Posy turned the iPod over in her hand, wondering what had become of that turntable and those albums. Madame Sylvie had suffered a sudden heart attack only three months after Posy had moved to San Francisco. In a single, tragic episode, both the ballet teacher and the school itself ceased to exist.

Posy had missed the funeral. She'd been dancing in her first real performance with the corps. *Swan Lake*, notorious for being the toughest ballet for corps dancers. It was the marathon of ballets. So while the woman who'd first taught her how to point her feet had been laid to rest, Posy had been fluttering across the stage in white feathers for three solid hours. By the end of the matinee that Saturday, her feet had hurt nearly as much as her heart.

Of all the things she'd missed in Aurora, Madame Sylvie's funeral was the one Posy had been the most conflicted about. Ultimately, she'd stayed in California because it was what her teacher would have wanted. Dancing that afternoon was the best way to honor Madame Sylvie's memory.

Posy had stitched a tiny black satin ribbon on the inside of her right pointe shoe in remembrance. And she'd danced until she no longer felt like crying.

A bittersweet smile came to Posy's lips as she clicked the iPod in place in the docking station. She hadn't thought about Madame Sylvie in a long time. Years maybe. This town was so full of memories, she was beginning to wonder if her heart had room for all of them.

And of course, just as she was feeling particularly wistful, the biggest memory of them all walked into the room.

"How's it going in here? Do you need any help?" Liam stood with his hands on his hips and looked around at the metal folding chairs lined up in neat rows up and down the length of the fellowship hall. "What are all the chairs for? I thought the girls were going to be dancing."

"The chairs are makeshift barres, for balance." Posy would have loved some full-length mirrors, like every actual ballet school had. But this wasn't a ballet school. It was a church. And anyway, this situation was temporary.

"Oh," Liam said, crossing his arms and scowling, clearly disappointed. As if she'd given up on teaching the girls ballet before they'd even started. "Well, do you need anything else?"

He glanced at the iPod in her hand, at the dance bag overflowing with tattered pointe shoes sitting at her feet and then at the chairs again. Was it Posy's imagination, or was he looking everywhere but at her injured foot?

It was the big, plaster-clad elephant in the room. She should have been relieved not to have to talk about it. But instead it irritated her that he was so painstakingly avoiding the topic. Then the fact that it irritated her just irritated her further.

"I think I've got things under control." She turned away from him and clicked the iPod in place on the player.

Prokofiev's *Peter and the Wolf* came blaring from the small speakers.

"Is this the music you're planning on using?" Liam's scowl morphed into a sardonic grin. Sarcasm aside, it was nice to see a smile on his face for a change. She hadn't seen him smile since she'd set foot in Alaska again.

She was surprised to realize that smile still brought a flutter to her belly.

It's nerves. That's all. Just nerves.

"Yes. Why? Is that a problem?" *Peter and the Wolf* had always been one of Posy's favorites. It was whimsical, with instruments representing each of the characters in the story. Oboe for the duck, clarinet for the cat, bassoon for the grandfather, the string instruments for Peter and the French horn for the wolf.

She'd loved it when she was a little girl. Madame Sylvie had played it in class only on rare special occasions. Posy figured this being the very first class definitely qualified.

"It's an odd choice." Liam let out a little laugh. "Don't you think?"

Posy's cheeks flushed. Was this what working with Liam was going to be like? Was he going to micromanage her music choices?

Peter and the Wolf was perfect. Liam was crazy if he

thought otherwise. What did he know about ballet anyway? This was the man who intentionally went out of his way to *not* know anything about dance. "What do you mean?"

He shrugged. "I don't know. Don't you think it's a little young? I mean, the girls…"

A deafening crash interrupted him before he could finish. The sound of metal on metal…on metal on metal on metal. And so on. The shock of it caused Posy to jump, and a lightning bolt of pain shot up her leg when she landed on her injured foot.

What in the world was going on? All the metal folding chairs she'd spent so much time arranging—dragging them out of the storage closet and lining them up all on her own so she wouldn't need to rely on Liam—were tumbling over, one against the other. It was like watching a falling line of dominoes.

"Great. Just great," Liam muttered, shaking his head.

Posy followed his gaze until she found the source of the catastrophe. The beast. She still couldn't quite wrap her mind around the fact that it was a dog.

She aimed a sideways glance at Liam. "I thought you said he wasn't unruly."

"I have it under control." His tone was anything but convincing.

She rolled her eyes. "I see that."

"Sorry. I'll fix it." He headed toward the row of overturned chairs and the dog, who'd dropped to the floor to writhe around on his back. Posy could have sworn she felt the ground shake beneath her feet. A mini, canine-triggered earthquake.

"Don't worry about it." She grabbed her crutches and hobbled her way past him as quickly as she could. She was actually growing pretty adept at using them, a fact that both thrilled and depressed her.

"Don't be silly. I can get them upright in no time." As if to demonstrate, he picked up a chair with one hand, and with a flick of his masculine wrist, it was back in its proper place.

"I'd rather do it myself." She swung her crutches in the direction of the next chair and began struggling with it while he stood there seething.

"Posy. Stop."

She jammed the chair on the floor. "Liam, you don't have to do this."

"Do what?" He crossed his arms and blocked her path to the next chair, forcing her to actually look at him.

She blinked. Good grief, he was handsome. She still couldn't wrap her head around it. Maybe she'd eventually get used to looking at those cool blue eyes that somehow seemed even bluer than they'd been six years ago. And he'd definitely grown taller. He had to look down to meet her gaze, just as he'd always had to do at the pond. Only he wasn't wearing ice skates now. He was flat-footed in dark brown hiking boots, arms crossed over his impressive chest.

Posy swallowed. When she thought about him, she still saw the boy she knew in high school, not this grown man whose intensity somehow made her heart skip a beat.

Lucky for her, that intensity also frustrated her to no end. "I know what you're doing, and it needs to stop."

"I'm setting up chairs in the fellowship hall. I work here, remember? It's my job. Didn't we cover this yesterday?"

"That's not what I'm talking about. Look, we both know what's going on here." She lifted her chin. Goodness, this situation was humbling. "You're babysitting me. And contrary to popular belief, I don't need a babysitter."

"You think I'm babysitting you?" He laughed. A little too loudly for Posy's liking.

"Yes. This—" she waved a hand back and forth between them "—is no coincidence. She told me about this job so you could keep an eye on me and make sure I don't... don't..."

Her mouth grew dry, and she couldn't quite force the words out.

Say it. Just say it.

My mother wants you to make sure I don't take any pills.

She cleared her throat. "You're watching me so I don't do anything stupid."

Way to be direct, Posy. She deflated a little. How could this still be so difficult to discuss after so long? Maybe because they'd never actually discussed it back then. Not really.

Liam stared at her through narrowed eyes. A muscle in his jaw twitched. "Is that what you're worried about?"

"Yes," she said quietly.

She'd suspected that was the case once she'd realized Liam was the youth pastor. And after she'd downed her fourth cup of coffee at the Northern Lights Inn the day before and finally headed home, the look on her mother's face had confirmed it.

"Well, you can rest easy, darling." *Darling.* Liam had called her that back when things had been perfect. Of course, back then the word hadn't dripped with obvious sarcasm as it did now.

"Are you denying that my mother expects you to keep an eye on me? Because I know that's the case. We talked about it last night."

"No, I'm not denying that at all. She point-blank asked me to look after you." His expression went distant. Cold. As cold as an Alaskan winter. "I turned her down flat. I'm not your keeper, Posy. Not anymore."

I'm not your keeper, Posy. Not anymore.

The words shouldn't have hurt, yet somehow they did.

"Good." She forced herself to smile. "Then we're in perfect agreement."

"Good," Liam echoed and went back to work straightening all of the chairs with exaggerated calmness.

As he did so, Posy tried her best to appear busy readying herself for class. But she felt like jumping out of her skin. She couldn't stand the care with which he resituated the chairs, setting each one down with barely a whisper of sound. The more composed he appeared, the more she felt as though she were coming undone. She wished he'd scream, yell, throw things. Anything to show that he was just as unnerved about this whole situation as she was.

She scrolled through her iPod, the songs blurring together as her mind went to a different place. A place she really didn't want to go, especially now as she was preparing to teach her first ballet class. But try as she might, she couldn't keep herself from imagining the conversation that had apparently taken place between Liam and her mother—her mother wringing anxious hands, that desperate look on her face that Posy could barely bring herself to look at.

And Liam.

Liam telling her parents he didn't want anything to do with her. This new Liam she didn't recognize. This Liam who wasn't really Liam.

The entire scenario should have made her angry. She was an adult now. She'd been enticed to return to Alaska under false pretenses, and her career was hanging in the balance all because she'd landed wrong on a simple arabesque that she'd done thousands of times before without incident. Her parents were trying to get her high school boyfriend to spy on her. She had every reason to be angry.

But she couldn't seem to muster much indignation. Because underneath all the agitation and embarrassment was the knowledge that Liam had become someone she no longer recognized because of her.

It had been raining that night. At first Posy had blamed the rain for what had happened. After she'd walked four blocks to the diner and called Liam for help, she'd been soaked to the bone. The cook had stood staring at her, frowning, as she'd clutched the pay phone, her shoes filling with the water dripping from her hair and her sodden clothes.

In the days, weeks and months that followed, she'd wondered if things would have turned out differently if she'd never called him that night. If she'd dialed her parents instead. It wasn't as if she'd have been able to hide the damage to her car. Or the tree, one of the oldest in Aurora. A blue spruce.

It had stood at the center of town, between the Northern Lights Inn and the skating pond. It still did. At least Posy assumed it was still there. When she'd met Anya and Zoey for coffee the day before, she'd intentionally taken a route that would allow her to avoid the moody blue tree. And the skating pond. And all the tender memories that swirled like fog over the ice.

Her parents would have found out eventually. Everyone had.

But in her panic, she'd called Liam. She hadn't been thinking about the tree when she'd made that fateful call. The fear pumping through her veins had prevented her from thinking about much of anything other than the fact that talking to her parents would be easier with Liam at her side, holding her hand. If she could just talk to him, see him, touch him, everything would be all right.

She couldn't have been more wrong.

"Posy, what is it? What's happened?" He knew something was wrong. Posy could hear the worry, the fear in his voice.

She tried her best to enunciate, to prevent her words from slurring. But her teeth were chattering so hard that trying to control what came out of her mouth was a fruitless endeavor.

"There's been an accident," she heard herself say.

It still didn't feel real. She kept thinking that maybe it wasn't. Maybe she was dreaming. Maybe morning would come, and she would open her eyes and find clear diamond skies. No rain. No pain. And no weeping sapphire tree.

"An accident. Are you okay?" He sounded calmer than she'd expected. As if he'd been waiting for such a call. Expecting it. As though he knew something like this was going to happen all along.

"Please come." She gripped the phone with all her might. She still felt light-headed from the pills. Even the impact of the tree hadn't been sufficient to eradicate the airy sensation in her limbs. She needed something to tether her to the ground, to keep her from floating away into oblivion. "Please."

There was an excruciating beat of silence before he said, "Tell me where you are."

"The big blue tree."

He hung up without a word.

She returned to her car to wait for him, unable to bear the scrutiny of the cook, the hostess and the patrons enjoying their burgers and milk shakes. Logically, she knew no one in the diner could tell what she'd done. To them, she was still the town good girl. The perfect music-box ballerina, dancing to an endless tune. Never falling.

She didn't want Liam to meet her there. She wanted to stay that town good girl for as long as possible. More than that, she wanted Liam to see her intact, unharmed, before he had a chance to catch sight of that horrible tangle of metal wrapped around the tree.

The wait was excruciating.

He arrived in a rumble of thunder and stepped from his car into the rain with an umbrella in his hands, but he made no effort to avoid the puddles at his feet. Pale, visibly shaken, he sloshed through ankle-deep water without taking his eyes off the wreckage.

Posy ran to him, placing herself between him and the tree. As if she could block the sight of it, prevent him from seeing all the damage she'd done.

"Posy," he whispered, as if it were the most melancholy word that had ever been spoken. Sadder than lonely, affliction and hopeless all put together.

Her name had never sounded that way falling from his lips. Hearing it frightened her just as bad as the accident had. Possibly even worse.

"I think I hydroplaned," she said, unable to quite meet Liam's gaze.

She stood there beneath the shelter of his umbrella, heart pounding in fear. Since the moment her car had swerved off the road and crashed into the tree, she'd been unable to take in a full breath. She wasn't hurt. At least she didn't think so. She just couldn't breathe, as if she were in a perpetual state of panic.

But as she stood under that umbrella and finally fixed her gaze on Liam, her fear turned to shame.

He knew.

She saw it in his desolate blue eyes. Eyes that always looked at her with a combination of wonder and affection. Eyes that suddenly went as moody blue as the evergreen in the storm.

His hair was soaked, rain running down his face in angry rivulets. Washing away all the lies. Everything she'd tried so hard to hide.

She had the fierce urge to reach out and chase the drops with her fingertips as they ran down his cheeks.

Heaven's tears. If she could just wipe them away, maybe all of this could be over. As if it had never happened.

"Let me see your purse," he said in a tone that sent a chill coursing through her.

"Why?" she asked through chattering teeth.

"You know why." His voice broke, and something inside Posy broke along with it. Not a bone, but something that would take far longer to heal. If it ever could.

"Liam, please."

"Let me see it. Now." The umbrella shook in Liam's hand, sending droplets of freezing rain skittering through the air. Dancing water, spinning into oblivion.

Her instinct was to grip her purse more tightly to her chest in case he tried to wrench it free. He never would do that, would he? Not Liam.

But the boy standing in front of her didn't quite look like Liam. She'd never seen that glint of fury in his eyes before. Not when she'd missed his eighteenth birthday party because she'd been in Portland auditioning for Oregon Ballet Theatre. Or when she'd missed the final baseball game of the season—the one where he'd scored the winning home run—because she'd had dance rehearsal. Or even when he'd walked in on her just that morning as she'd cradled a tiny blue capsule in her hand in the quiet, desperate moment before she tossed it back with a swallow of water.

She let the strap of her bag slide from her shoulder, down her arm, and held her purse limply toward him, praying he wouldn't take it. Hoping against hope he was bluffing.

He wasn't. He took her bag, exchanging it for the umbrella handle. It took him only moments to find what he was looking for. Three pill bottles, one of them empty, the other two half-full, jammed into the toes of the pointe shoes she never went anywhere without.

He shook them loose, until the bottles fell into his palm. Then he stared down at them, motionless, until his fist closed around the clear orange plastic. His knuckles went white, his grip so tight that it looked as though he were trying to crush them with his bare hands.

"How long?" he asked, his voice barely audible above the pounding rain.

It was coming down in buckets then. Rain like Posy had never seen before. Like something out of a Shakespeare play. The Tempest.

"Not long." Posy tried to swallow, but she couldn't make her body work anymore. First her feet, now her throat. She knew her heart would be the next to rebel. "Only a few days."

He closed his eyes, his eyelashes inky dark, dripping with rainwater against his ghostly face. "Don't lie to me, Posy."

She needed him to look at her, to see that she was the same girl she'd always been. But that wasn't quite true, was it? The girl he loved didn't do things like this.

Everything started slipping from her grip. She held on so tightly—as tightly as Liam gripped those awful bottles of pills. But she still wasn't able to hang on. Her body was failing her just when she'd needed it most. Even the pills weren't working anymore. Not as well as they had in the beginning.

Every day it was harder and harder to dance. She was losing ballet. She felt it as surely as she felt the broken bone in her foot.

The thought of losing Liam too was inconceivable.

"Six weeks," she whispered, knowing she couldn't lie. Not to him. "I've been taking them for six weeks. Only one a day at first."

"More lately, though."

"More, yes." She prayed he wouldn't press for further

details. It was too embarrassing. She wasn't even able to bring herself to think about it, much less say it out loud.

But he pressed on, insisting that she tell him how many she'd taken that day. How many and at what times. She answered his questions as honestly as she could, but it was difficult to concentrate. Her head was so fuzzy. So much of the day was nothing but a blur.

"Where did you get them?" he asked.

There was no use lying. The information was printed right there on the prescription labels.

"From my parents' medicine cabinet. They're left over from my dad's back surgery last year. I'll put them back. I promise. Just as soon as my auditions are over." She reached for the pills with a tentative hand.

He closed his fist around the pill bottles and jerked his arm away from her. And in a moment of slow-motion agony that she would never forget, her ballet shoes tumbled from her bag.

Posy sank to her knees a moment too late. Her precious pointe shoes landed in a puddle, ribbons streaming in a rush of rainwater. Priceless pink satin. Ruined. As surely as her future. She gathered them to her chest. Crushed them against her breaking heart.

"Posy, darling. It's already over," Liam whispered.

"No." She shook her head, unable to hear what he was saying. "No, it's not."

She still had one more audition left. The most important of them all—the Pacific Northwest Ballet in Seattle. The one closest to home.

"Yes, it is. You could have hurt someone tonight, Posy. You could have been killed." Liam fixed his gaze on hers. Finally. And she realized he was right.

It was over. All of it. From the moment she'd hit that tree.

"Ballet." He said it as if it were a dirty word. Some-

thing awful and vile. Something to be ashamed of. "It's not worth your life, Posy."

But it is.

She very nearly said those words, but caught herself in time.

He never would understand. No one would. She didn't understand it herself. All she knew was that she'd dreamed of being a dancer for as long as she could remember. She couldn't conceive of doing anything else. The very idea of losing the thing she loved most in the world filled her with panic.

Truth be told, it still did.

Although she wasn't going to stoop to such desperate measures this time. This time, she was committed to doing things right. She would fly to Anchorage for her doctor's appointments. She'd rest. She'd elevate her foot at night. She'd stay away from pills that would do nothing but mask the pain and place her once again on that dangerous slope toward losing control.

This time, she would pray.

She squeezed her eyes shut in an effort to keep the memories at bay. She didn't want to remember. Not here. Not now, while Liam was less than twenty feet away.

But memory was an unrelenting dance partner.

She could close her eyes against the past, but she could still see herself standing, clutching her ruined ballet slippers to her heart, unable to let go of the dream. She could still feel the mud caked onto her knees, feel the frigid water dripping down her legs.

"You're going to tell my parents." It was a statement rather than a question. The answer was written all over Liam's face.

"I have to, Posy. It's the only way I know to help you."

He stared at the muddy ballet shoes in a way that made her crush them more tightly to her chest.

"I thought you were on my side," she protested.

"I am. We all are. Can't you see that?"

"Please, Liam. Please. Don't. I'm begging you. Please."
She shook from head to toe. Frozen. Wet. Panicked.

In another place, in another time, Liam would wrap his arms around her to warm her. He would give her his coat and hold her until the trembling stopped.

He'd always been protective of her. He always carried her schoolbooks, offered her his letter jacket, held her hand when they skated.

He was protecting her then, too. But somehow it still felt like an unimaginable betrayal.

"If you tell them, I'll never speak to you again. Never." She didn't mean it. It was just something to say. Something to stop him.

She hadn't meant it. She hadn't.

But in the end, it had been the one and only promise to him that she'd kept.

Chapter Six

Liam wasn't interested in chivalry.

He really wasn't. He was simply doing his job.

He ignored Posy's protests and continued lining up all the chairs that his dog had knocked over. If it made her angry, that was just too bad. Let her stew. He might not have signed on as her babysitter, but it would have been silly to let her do it herself. He could get it done in a fraction of the time, seeing as he was able-bodied and she was injured.

Plus he just wanted her to stay put. He couldn't stand watching her move around on those crutches. She reminded him of a wobbly baby giraffe trying to take its first steps. It was an image in such striking opposition to her usual grace and poise that it caused an uncomfortable ache in his chest. An ache that felt oddly like pity.

He didn't want to feel pity for Posy...for *Josephine*. He didn't want to feel anything for her.

He set the final chair in its place, frowned and moved it a fraction of an inch so that it stood perfectly in line with the rest of the row. He clenched his fists at his sides. Every cell in his body longed to pick up that chair and heave it out the closest window. Having Posy around was even more difficult than he'd imagined. But he wasn't about to let the chaos of his emotions show.

It's only temporary. Just grin and bear it. Before long, this will all be over. She'll dance right out of Alaska... again.

He took a measured inhalation and spun around to face her. "All right. Looks like you're set to go."

"You didn't have to do that." Her tone was crisp, and she kept her eyes glued to her iPod. "But...thank you."

"You're welcome." He crossed his arms.

Now what?

"Are those bears for the girls?" He nodded at the teddy bears she'd lined up against the wall.

"Yes. I thought they might like them. Those silly bears were still lining the shelves of my bedroom. Can you imagine? After all this time." She shook her head. "Nothing changes around here, does it?"

She smiled brightly. A perfectly staged grin. But he could see a hint of uncertain melancholy in those familiar eyes. Things had changed. *Everything* had changed. She knew that just as well as he did.

He shook his head. "Nope. I suppose not."

Why did he get the sense that they were dancing together in a broken time capsule every time they looked at one another? And when would it stop?

"I should probably finish getting ready." She gestured with her iPod toward a bag overflowing with pale pink ballet shoes.

He had to give her credit. She'd come prepared. She was obviously taking the job seriously. More seriously than he would have guessed. But honestly, how serious could she be when she had no intention of sticking around once she could dance again?

"About the music...and the bears..." He jammed his hand through his hair.

She bristled. The delicate gossamer thread of connection that had found its way between them tore as easily as a spiderweb. "What about them?"

He wanted to tell her to rethink the music because that *Peter and the Wolf* selection wasn't going to go over well at all. He had his suspicions about the teddy bears, as well. Bears in ballet shoes.

"I appreciate the effort, but…"

"It's for the girls. Not you." She wrapped her arms around her slender form. She was dressed in long black leggings and thick-knit leg warmers up to her thighs, paired with a leotard layered with a pale pink wraparound sweater, and still she shivered. She'd always been that way. Hands cold to the touch, forever seeking warmth. Perhaps it was best she'd left Alaska after all. "The effort, I mean. I know you don't want me here. You tried to get me fired."

"Not fired. Unhired." He cleared his throat. "Technically."

The way she put it made it sound so awful. In retrospect, perhaps it was. Still, she couldn't possibly feel any more comfortable with the situation than he did.

"Same thing. So I think it's best if you do your job and I do mine." She turned her back, effectively dismissing him.

Liam stayed put for a moment, transfixed by the back of her willowy neck, exposed by her upswept copper hair.

"About the music, though," he said, giving it one last try.

She didn't say a word, didn't turn around, just kept moving in that graceful way she always had. It was then, when he could watch her, really look at her unobserved, that he realized how much he'd missed the way the simple turn of a sinuous wrist could make his breath catch in his throat.

He closed his eyes. His head hurt all of a sudden. "Never

mind. School lets out in ten minutes. I'll be outside with
the boys if you need anything." He nodded in the direction of the field beside the church, which in his tenure as
youth pastor had served as a baseball diamond, summer
fairground, soccer field, football practice lawn and now
site of the impending snowball battle.

"Okay. Thanks." She glanced at him over her shoulder.
Just for a moment.

He promptly looked away. "See you later, then."

Mature. Really mature.

He shook his head as he grabbed his parka and headed
outside. This was ridiculous. They were acting like teenagers, nearly as ridiculous as Ronnie and Melody. What
a fine example they'd set for the kids.

Lord, where are You in all this?

Silence.

He pushed through the church's heavy double doors,
out into the cold. The temperature had dipped even lower
than expected. The icy wind bit at his face and sent a sharp
icicle breeze through his hair. He dragged a skullcap from
the pocket of his parka and pulled it on.

"Nothing?" His gaze shot skyward. Dove-gray clouds,
heavy with snow, were draped so low that it almost felt as
though they were pressing down on him, barely skimming
the top of his head. Afternoons were never particularly
bright this time of year in Aurora, as the sun typically set
early. Sometimes as early as four o'clock. But this sky was
different. Swollen with secrets. A storm waiting to happen. "Because now would be a great time for a sign, no
matter how small. Anything to let me know You're aware
of what's going on down here."

He waited a beat, then blew out a breath he hadn't realized he'd been holding. It hung in the air, suspended in
a cloud of icy vapor.

Grow up. The world is full of problems far bigger than yours.

He dropped his gaze from the sky.

And was promptly hit square in the face with a wet, sloppy snowball.

He was stunned for a moment, frozen in place. He hadn't seen it coming. Aside from a painfully throbbing nose, his face had gone numb from the cold. Snow was everywhere. In his eyes, his nose, his mouth. If he hadn't just put on his hat, he would have had two earfuls of it, as well.

You asked for a sign, and everybody knows the Lord works in mysterious ways.

He swallowed a mouthful of slush and wiped the mess from his eyes. He blinked a few times and found seven familiar faces staring back at him, wearing expressions of amusement mixed with the smallest possible dash of sympathy.

"Heads up, Pastor." Ronnie, the perpetual leader of the pack, grinned and tossed another snowball back and forth between his hands.

Liam reached for it, snatching it midair.

"*Now* you give me a heads-up?" He reminded himself that he loved these teenagers. Every last snowball-wielding one of them. "Shouldn't that have come a minute or two earlier?"

"All's fair in love and war, right, Pastor?" Ethan Locklear, the gangliest of the bunch at six feet tall and one hundred forty-five pounds soaking wet, shrugged. "And this snowball business is war, right?"

All's fair in love and war. Since when did the boys quote sixteenth-century English writers?

Ronnie rolled his eyes. "We're studying poetry at school."

That explained things.

All's fair in love and war.

Love.

War.

He preferred the latter. Less dangerous.

Posy heard her new ballet students before she had a chance to get a glimpse of them. How could she not? Their footsteps echoed in the hallway with all the grace of a herd of wild musk oxen. Giggles bounced off the walls. And yelling. So much yelling.

Posy swallowed. She couldn't remember any of Madame Sylvie's classes being anywhere near this noisy. Then again, maybe she wasn't remembering things all that accurately. She'd been a little girl herself when she'd first stepped into a ballet studio. Five years old. Barely more than a baby. Maybe kids were always this loud.

The commotion grew closer. An approaching blizzard.

Posy's throat went dry. Her heartbeat kicked up a notch like it always did in the final moments before the red velvet curtain was lifted. She felt the same way she had so many times before, suspended in those enchanting seconds of darkness, bathed in shadows, waiting in breathless anticipation for the warm glow of the spotlight. Mere seconds that inevitably lasted a lifetime.

Stage fright.

What had she gotten herself into? She knew plenty about ballet. She knew *everything* about ballet. But what did she really know about teaching? Or children?

Nothing.

She had the sudden urge to grab one of the teddy bears she'd brought for the girls and curl up on the floor in the fetal position.

Don't be ridiculous. You can do this. Little girls love anything to do with ballet. Piece of cake.

Posy squared her shoulders and adopted her onstage posture—chin lifted ever so slightly, ramrod-straight spine. She reminded herself, once again, that this was only temporary. What was the worst that could happen?

The door from the hallway flew open, and in walked her students. But wait…they weren't her students after all. They were adults.

Or were they?

"Hi," the tiniest one said. She had the slim, delicate build of a dancer. Posy could see it, even beneath the layers of winter clothing. A backpack bursting at the seams with the solid square shapes of books slid from her shoulders and landed on the floor with a thud.

The metal folding chairs Liam had so carefully arranged jumped in place.

"Are you the ballet teacher?" another one of them asked, her skeptical gaze skipping over Posy's dance clothes and zeroing in on her injured foot.

And then the questions came at her from every direction. All at once, with the dizzying speed of a fouetté turn. So fast and furious that Posy couldn't keep track of them all.

"What happened to your leg?"

"Are you hurt?"

"Did that happen doing ballet?"

"Are those *teddy bears*?"

"Can you even dance with that cast on your foot?"

"Is ballet dangerous?"

That last one she'd heard. She sent up a silent prayer of thanks that Liam was outside somewhere throwing snowballs and hadn't been around to hear it, too.

"What is this crazy music?" the small one with the two-ton backpack asked, prompting the others to erupt in a fit of giggles.

Posy stumbled toward her iPod docking station, forgoing the crutches altogether and simply dragging her plaster foot behind her. She managed to slam the power button just as Peter was about to encounter the lilting, whimsical clarinet tune of the cat.

The laughter died along with Prokofiev.

Posy cleared her throat. "That was *Peter and the Wolf.* It's a classic, actually. But never mind about that."

Two of the girls dragged a couple of folding chairs closer and slumped into them. So much for Posy's make-shift ballet barre.

She pasted on a smile. "Great idea. Why don't we all sit down? We can have a little chat and get acquainted."

She took a seat in the chair she'd intended to use as her instructional barre, hating the way her leg looked stick-ing out straight in front of her in its cast. Foot immobile. Permanently flexed. It pained her not to be able to point her toes.

But she had more important things to think about at the moment. She needed to regroup. *Obviously.* These weren't children at all. These were teenagers.

Posy cleared her throat and tried to wrap her mind around the current state of affairs. She'd made a mistake. An as-sumption. But it wasn't the end of the world. She would just have to regroup, that was all.

"So…" She pasted on a smile. "My name is Josephine Sutton, but you can call me Posy."

She'd planned on asking them to call her Madame Jo-sephine in the spirit of her old ballet teacher. But that sounded ridiculous spinning around in her imagination right now, faced with a roomful of adolescent girls. Ado-lescent girls dressed in street clothes—jeans, heavy sweat-ers and snow boots. Not a leotard in sight.

Posy's pink-and-black ensemble seemed silly and pre-sumptuous all of a sudden. "I'm a dancer with the West Coast Arts Ballet Company in San Francisco. A soloist." Soon-to-be principal dancer. *Please, God.* "But for now, I'm here in Aurora to teach ballet."

"Why?" one of the girls asked.

"Why?" Posy repeated, stalling while she tossed different answers around in her head.

Because I have nowhere else to go. Because I can't spend entire days at my parents' house with my mother watching me as if I might shatter and break into a million pieces. Because without dance, I'm lost.

"Because I love ballet, and I want to share that love with you." There. That sounded good, and it was the truth.

Mostly. The rest of the story was far too complicated to explain to a group of strangers. Particularly strangers who were beginning to look as bored as if they were listening to a Mahler score. The girl with the enormous backpack seemed to be the only one paying attention.

She appeared to be studying Posy with unusual intensity. "I meant, why here? Why Aurora?"

"Oh." A simple question. Good. "I grew up here. I graduated from Aurora High, then moved to San Francisco to dance."

Backpack girl piped up again. Posy got the impression she was the group's unofficial leader. "Did you know Pastor Liam?"

Pastor Liam.

Posy held back an eye roll. "Yes. We went to school together."

"Did you ever date?" This was followed by a collective eruption of giggles.

Posy squirmed in her chair/makeshift barre. She'd been back in town for two days and a ballet teacher for a grand total of ten minutes, and already she was being questioned about her romantic history with Liam by kids she didn't even know. "That's not important."

The girls exchanged bemused glances.

"That means *yes*," one of them said.

"No." Posy shook her head. "It doesn't. It means it's not important. My friendship with Pastor Liam has nothing to do with ballet, which is why we're here."

Her *friendship* with Liam? That was a stretch.

All of a sudden a profound sadness wrapped itself around her. They'd once been everything to each other. And now it felt like a lie to even call him her friend.

Her face felt hot. It was probably twenty-five degrees outside, and she was sweating. *Please, God. No more questions.*

"What happened to your foot?"

That again. She wished her injury could be invisible, even for just a day. Twenty-four hours without that dreadful cast taking center stage would have been pure bliss. "I fell onstage and broke a bone in my foot."

"Does it hurt?"

More than I can possibly say. "Not too much."

Once more, they all started speaking at the same time, peppering her with questions.

"How long until it gets better?"

"When can you dance again?"

"Will you be able to do all the same things you could do before? Leaps and turns and stuff?"

It was like having a chorus sing her every unspoken fear aloud. She had to resist the urge to cover her ears.

"I'm going to be fine. Soon." *I hope.* "Okay, it's my turn to ask the questions now. Let's start with your names."

The tiny outspoken one with the enormous backpack was called Melody, and the others were Ava, Rachel, Hannah, Emily, Madison and Darcy.

With the notable exception of Melody, who probably had a future in television or politics, the girls were much more soft-spoken when answering questions than when doling them out. Posy had to strain to hear a few of their names.

She began to breathe a little easier. "How many of you have taken ballet lessons before?"

The girls exchanged glances. Not a single hand went up.

"None of you?" Posy made a valiant effort not to let her disappointment show.

By the time she'd reached her teens, Posy had worn out more ballet shoes than she could count. Granted, she'd had Madame Sylvie. These girls had no one.

A lump lodged in her throat. Aurora was a town without a ballet school. Girls who grew up here never had the opportunity to stand on tiptoe in front of a mirrored wall and dream about leaping and turning across a stage in a fluffy tutu and glittering tiara. They never dressed in black leotards and candy-pink tights or knew the secret thrill of watching their arabesques grow higher year after year.

Posy found this even more difficult to digest than the fact that Liam was a pastor.

She'd taken the loss of Madame Sylvie so personally that she'd never thought about what it had meant for her hometown. What it had meant for all the little girls who blew out candles on birthday cakes decorated with little plastic ballerina cake toppers. There would be no *The Nutcracker* at Christmastime, no spring recital. No rites of passage such as the first fluffy tutu, the first pair of shiny satin pointe shoes or dancing a pas de deux with a partner for the first time.

No pointed toes, no pink tights, no ballerina buns. No pliés, no relevés, no piqué turns. Not one girl in this room, this town would ever curtsy on a stage laden with long-stemmed roses.

Aurora had become a place that ballet had forgotten.

You're here now. You can remind them. At least for a while.

She stood and planted her hands on her hips, much like the way Madame Sylvie had always done. "Stand up, girls. It's time to get to work."

Chapter Seven

Midway through practice, the boys were so covered with snow that Liam could hardly tell them apart. This was somewhat disconcerting, considering the object of the sport was to avoid getting hit. On the other hand, he supposed their general state of disarray also meant they were getting good at hitting their intended targets.

At present, the practice session had become a head-to-head battle between Ronnie and another of the boys, Caleb White. According to the official rules of competitive snowballing, once a team member was hit three times, he was out. Unless the team member was a female, in which case the number of hits went up to five. Seeing as Liam's attempts at recruiting the girls had been such a spectacular failure, that particular fact was irrelevant.

"You're going down, Ronnie!" Caleb's head popped out from behind the barrier he'd been crouching behind. In real games—such as the one on the schedule for Saturday—against real teams, large orange plastic barriers scattered the playing field. Liam, of course, didn't have official barriers, but he had trash cans. They did the trick just fine, so long as Sundog didn't knock them over first.

After a few fake-outs, Caleb flung a snowball in Ronnie's direction. It whizzed right past the intended target's head. Ronnie let out a laugh and returned fire with a snowball of his own, which slammed against the trash can with a wet thud.

Liam's dog sat at his feet, ears pricked forward, head swiveling back and forth as he followed the trajectory of the flying snowballs. It had taken only an hour or so for Liam to stop him from chasing each and every one. He really needed to get a handle on the training situation. Wearing him out wasn't working, because Sundog outlasted Liam each and every time.

Caleb's head peeked out from behind the trash can for a split second. So quickly that Liam wasn't altogether sure he hadn't imagined it.

He glanced at the stopwatch in his hand. "Remember, you can only stay behind the barrier for twenty seconds at a time. The referee will keep track."

Caleb dashed from one trash can to the next, narrowly dodging a flurry of frantically tossed snowballs.

"Ronnie, slow down and aim. You only have a limited number of snowballs." One thousand per team, to be exact. Seventy percent of which they'd used within the first ten minutes of practice. That didn't even include the 10 percent that had been devoured by the dog.

Liam harbored little hope for a victory. Not that it mattered. The boys were having a blast. At the end of every practice, they went home happily exhausted, with huge grins on their snow-covered faces. But it would be nice to show up on Saturday and not get completely annihilated within the first few minutes of the game.

"Your time behind that trash can is running out again, Caleb." Liam looked back down at his stopwatch. "Three… two…one…"

A yell came from the ranks of the boys watching from the sidelines. "Wait! You can't go out there."

Liam looked up from the stopwatch to find that the number of people out on the field had suddenly gone from two to three. One member of the trio was marching in his direction. On crutches.

Posy.

Woof. Sundog rose to his feet.

"Settle down," Liam muttered. He couldn't blame the dog, really. He felt rather like letting out a defensive bark himself at the sight of her charging toward him like that.

He sighed. "Posy, you shouldn't be out here."

"We need to talk," she shouted from midfield.

Liam shook his head. "Not now. And most definitely not here."

Caleb and Ronnie took a few shots at each other. Liam winced as the snowballs zipped past Posy. She trod on, oblivious, jamming her crutches in the newly fallen powder.

"Please stop, Posy. Please. Just turn around." Liam held out a hand in the universal sign for *stop*, which she promptly ignored. Naturally.

The boys were taking full advantage of the distraction, flinging snowballs fast and furiously. One of them skimmed the top of Posy's head, frosting her ballerina bun.

This was going to end badly. Liam could feel it.

Sure enough, she took another step, and one of her crutches hit an icy patch and nearly slid out from under her. She squealed, righted herself and kept on coming.

Liam's gut twisted. He was going to end up with an ulcer the size of Alaska by the time Posy left town. Had she always had this maddening effect on him?

No. Maybe. Yes.

Once upon a time, you liked it.

If that was true, then he'd been the mad one. Certifiable.

"Posy. Stop. Right now," he said through gritted teeth. She responded by hastening her wobbly steps.

Super. He was going to have to go after her. She'd given him no choice. He threw the stopwatch on the ground and marched across the field, torn between hoping he reached her before she went down and wanting her to fall spectacularly on her stubborn backside. Sundog scurried after him in a flurry of snow and wooly paws.

"Pastor?" Ronnie said, a note of bewilderment in his tone, as Liam walked by.

"Finally you take your eye off the ball." Caleb aimed right for Ronnie's head.

"Think again, bro." Ronnie laughed and dodged behind Posy.

Liam became even more aware of his ulcer-in-waiting. He stopped in front of Posy and pretended to ignore the fact that she was noticeably out of breath. From going twenty feet or so on crutches in the snow. He couldn't remember ever seeing Posy out of breath before, even after one of her dance recitals. She could skate laps around him at the pond, pirouetting and twirling around him as if he'd been standing still. She'd never broken a sweat. Her body was a machine.

"What do you think you're doing? In case you haven't noticed, we're in the middle of practice." He threw his arms up just as his point was further emphasized by a pair of snowballs crisscrossing in the air between them.

"You didn't tell me." She glared at him so hard that he wondered if he should be more concerned about getting hit by one of her crutches than snowball shrapnel.

"Didn't tell you what?" He knew what, and he supposed he should have expected her angry reaction. But he'd tried to tell her. He really had. She just hadn't wanted to listen.

"They're teenagers, Liam." She waved a crutch toward the girls chatting animatedly as they exited the building and began gathering on the sidelines alongside the boys who'd been eliminated earlier in the match.

At the sudden appearance of Melody on the scene, Ronnie's movements on the field became more exaggerated, his taunts to Caleb even louder. Liam tried to remember why he'd ever thought becoming a youth pastor had been a good idea. "Yes, I know they're teenagers. And you would have known that, too, if you'd paid attention to my advice."

"Is this about the song?" A snowball whooshed toward Posy's face. Liam winced, certain of impact, but she ducked in the nick of time. *Nice reflexes.* "You always hated that song. *Always.*"

It wasn't the song he'd hated. Just as he hadn't hated the pointe shoes that had always been nestled in the bottom of her bag or the black leotards that she'd always worn beneath her sweaters. The trappings had never truly bothered him.

It had been dance itself. The way she lit up when she talked about it. The way the utterance of those two syllables—*bal-let*—would drip from her tongue sweeter than the sugar cubes they'd liked to feed to the reindeer on Gus Henderson's farm.

Even ballet he couldn't bring himself to hate entirely. He'd thought he did, until he'd seen her dance for the first time. It hadn't been a real performance, or even rehearsal. She'd simply been practicing. Alone, in a mirrored room at her dance studio while she waited for him to pick her up and take her to one of his baseball games. He'd walked through the door and stopped dead in his tracks. Captivated. Entranced. Utterly spellbound by the way she'd moved.

Balanced on her toes, so fragile yet at the same time so strong. Every sinewy muscle in her lithe legs had been stretched taut. And there'd been unspeakable grace in the tension.

He'd never seen anything, anyone, so beautiful. On and

on she'd danced, oblivious to his presence, her pink-slippered feet turning so fast they were a blur. Tiptoe twirls punctuated with sudden leaps. The languid placement of an arm, the butterfly flutter of fingertips. Her every movement had been a blushing kiss upon the air.

She hadn't been moving in response to the music. She'd been having a conversation with it. A conversation beyond all words. A conversation in which Liam had been nothing more than an accidental observer. An eavesdropper.

Yet how could he hate it—the exquisite gift she'd been given? He couldn't. Not then. Not even now. Posy Sutton had been born to dance.

"I never hated the song," he said. *"Peter and the Wolf."*

She rolled her eyes. "Sure you didn't."

It wasn't so much a song as a compilation of noises. A story told with instruments, with occasional bursts of melody. The collection of string instruments that represented Peter got a little old after a while. As did the high-pitched flute of the birds.

Liam sighed. "Okay, maybe it wasn't my favorite, but that didn't have anything to do with this morning. I tried to tell you to choose something else."

"But you didn't tell me why. You just let me assume I'd been hired to teach little girls."

He narrowed his gaze at her. "Let's talk about that for a minute, shall we? You traveled all the way here from San Francisco to teach ballet, and it never occurred to you to ask Pastor McNeil...*Lou*...the ages of the girls in the program?"

Her glare lost a bit of its defiance. "It didn't exactly come up in conversation."

A snowball arched high above their heads. Posy's gaze followed its movement, but Liam's eyes never left hers. There was something different about those eyes. They'd always been stormy. The eyes of a girl who wanted more.

But that agitated hunger looked as though it had been tempered somehow, replaced with what could only be described as melancholy.

It didn't sit well with Liam. "Posy, just what was going on back in California that made you anxious to leave?"

"What? Nothing. Everything is fine back in San Francisco. More than fine, actually."

Then why did you just say back in San Francisco *instead of back* home?

It wasn't his business. It wasn't his business, nor did he want it to be. "If you say so."

"I do say so. Once my foot heals, I'm getting promoted to principal."

"Yes, you mentioned that." What she hadn't mentioned was a boyfriend, or any friends, for that matter. No social life at all. Only ballet. Always ballet.

"Stop changing the subject." She blew a stray tendril of copper from her eyes. Liam fought the nonsensical urge to tuck it behind her ear. "You knew I expected little girls. You should have said something. You're the youth pastor."

As if he needed reminding.

Caleb sidestepped a snowball and returned fire, tossing one after another as quickly as his arms could move. Ronnie darted in circles, slipping and sliding in the snow, but somehow successfully avoiding getting hit. Liam would have complimented him on his agility had he not been standing in the middle of what was beginning to look like Caleb's last stand. Ronnie wasn't about to surrender victory while Melody was watching.

Snowballs whizzed past. Sundog barked and snapped, trying to catch them in his formidable jaws. Posy shied away. What was it with her and the dog? He was harmless. He wanted to eat some snow, not devour ballerinas.

"Uh-oh. Look out!" someone yelled. Caleb? Ronnie? One of the other boys?

It didn't matter. It was too little, too late. Posy took another step backward, away from Sundog, and ended up getting pelted on the left ear by a snowball.

"Ouch!" She screamed and reached to brush the snow away from her face, and in a moment of slow-motion action-movie terror, Liam watched her crutches fall out from under her.

Her arms windmilled in the air, and he reached out to catch her before she fell. But quicker than his hands could find her, a snowball hit him in the dead center of his chest, knocking the wind out of him.

He bent over and tried to catch his breath as Posy collapsed in a pile. "Boys, we need to take five, okay?" he wheezed.

But his voice was barely audible, and the snowballs continued to fly. What little sound Liam could make was drowned out by Sundog's frenzied barks as he launched himself at every snowball that came his way.

Liam coughed and gulped at the air. He needed to breathe. Pronto. Posy hadn't moved a muscle since she'd gone down, as far as he could tell. She was bent over herself, sitting on the ground, facing the opposite direction. All he could see was her back and her disassembled ballerina bun, her auburn hair loose in the snow. Fire and ice.

He cleared his throat, coughed again and managed to take in his first deep inhalation. "Posy, are you okay?" Nothing. "Posy?"

He took a tentative step toward her.

She stirred ever so slightly. And then, quicker than he could process what was happening, she turned and aimed a perfectly packed snowball right at his head.

Posy knew it was a cheap shot. Even good old-fashioned snowball fights, the sort of impromptu battles fought on schoolyard playgrounds rather than official playing fields, had a certain etiquette. Intentionally aiming at someone's face surely breached some sort of unwritten rule. But it felt so good to throw that snowball at Liam's head.

So very good.

And it felt even better when the kids started whooping and hollering. The girls seemed to find it hilarious, but the boys were a different story. All action on the field ceased. Even Liam's lunatic dog had gone still. The two teens that just moments ago had seemed intent on annihilating one another were now standing with their mouths agape, shaking their heads.

"Oh, burn!" one of them said.

"You got served, Pastor." The other one jammed his hands on his hips. "You're not going to let her get away with that, are you?"

Liam wiped the snow from his face, ignored the kids and lifted a wet, angry brow at Posy. "I overlooked it when you maced me, but this is different."

"How so?" she asked, feigning calm as she righted herself on her crutches and stood. Something had been let loose inside her, and it was unraveling. If it had been visible, it would have resembled pink satin ribbons spilling from her heart onto the glistening snow.

"Oh, I don't know. Over the course of the past few days I've been sprayed in the eyes with Aqua Net and taken two cheap snowball shots to the face. I suppose I've reached my limit." He bent, scooped up a generous handful of snow and began methodically packing it into a tight ball.

"You're not going to hit me with that, are you?" she asked, pushing her wet hair from her eyes.

Oh, but that was exactly what he was going to do. She knew it. The kids knew it. Even the ridiculous dog knew it.

"Yes, I am." He smoothed the snowball and held it in his open palm, letting it taunt her as it glistened in the sun. "Do you know why?"

Posy's hands shook, and her heart beat as if there were a wild bird trapped inside. "Do enlighten me."

"Because that's what happens in a *snowball fight*!" It was nothing short of a battle cry, and as he let the snowball go, the kids charged onto the field, yelling, hollering and scooping up snow in a frenzy of winter madness.

The dog seemed to be everywhere at once, barking and bounding through the snow, his massive, wagging tail flinging fresh white powder over anyone within ten feet.

Posy ducked. Liam's snowball flew overhead, as did about a dozen more. She clawed at the snow, her fingertips going numb. When a wet mass of snow hit her shoulder, she all but gave up on forming balls and simply threw handfuls of snow in Liam's direction.

She had no idea how many, if any, made contact. She could barely see. The air was a blinding fog of snow swirling amid echoes of teenage laughter. For a moment, time seemed to move backward. She'd been here before. In this same field. Tossing snowballs. Laughing, tumbling on the snowy ground in Liam's arms. Years ago. Before everything had gone so horribly wrong.

Before the pain.

Before the rain.

How long had it been since she'd been in an actual snowball fight? She couldn't remember. Snow wasn't exactly commonplace in San Francisco. Neither was free time. Time to just *be*. She always had someplace to go, something to do. Dress rehearsals, fittings, dance practice. Barre classes. So many barre classes over the years that she couldn't begin to guess how many. Yoga, to keep her muscles stretched and loose. Ice baths. Epsom-salt baths. Anything and everything to keep her body dancing.

And stretching. She was always stretching. When she wasn't stretching at the barre or on the smooth wood floor of the studio, bathed in light from windows that led to a world she'd forgotten even existed, she was stretching on the floor of her apartment while watching television. Or in her kitchen, an oddly perfect place, as the countertop was within an inch of barre height. She even stretched at the supermarket. Or practiced her barre exercises. Relevés while holding on to her grocery cart. Tendus in the checkout line. Arms moving automatically through a complete port de bras while reaching for the canned soup.

Every moment of her life was somehow choreographed into a dance. She'd forgotten what it felt like to use her body for anything else.

A snowball hit her in the back, and she wobbled in the shin-deep snow. Her crutches lay forgotten, tossed at odd angles on the ground. She needed her hands for more important things at the moment, although she'd all but lost feeling in her fingers. Even her feet were going numb. The muscles in her arms burned from the unfamiliar motion of all the throwing. But it was a delicious burn. The burn of movement.

She heaved snow at anyone she could see. She'd completely lost track of Liam in the frenzy. But she could feel his presence in every snowflake. And for the first time since she'd been back, she didn't shy away from it. She simply lifted her face to the sky and let the snow dance coolly against her skin.

She was home. She was doing something that had nothing to do with dance. For the briefest of moments, she was inexplicably happy. Full of the kind of joy she hadn't realized she'd been missing.

Until Melody Tucker ran past, tripped over one of the discarded crutches and slammed into Posy's side. In an instant, the beautiful snow-globe world came crashing to a shattering end. Posy twisted to the ground, her body going one direction as her injured foot stayed facing another, unable to move, anchored in the snow by the weight of her plaster cast and all the dreams she wasn't ready to give up.

Chapter Eight

"**P**astor! Help! *Pastor!*"

Liam knew something was wrong the moment he heard Melody's screams. There was a panic in her voice that went beyond games and playing in the snow.

"Melody?" He dropped the snowball he'd been holding. "Where are you?"

He couldn't see a thing. The kids were all over the place, and a thick layer of white hung in the air, obscuring everything. He was standing in the middle of a snowstorm, being assaulted on every side. "Everyone, stop. Please."

He used a voice he'd never used before with the kids. One that he'd never wanted to use. But it worked.

Everyone came to a standstill, and through the swirling snow, he spotted Melody. She appeared to be perfectly fine. Still standing. Uninjured, as far as Liam could tell. Relief skittered through him. Then he spotted a figure at Melody's feet, and his heart stopped.

Posy.

He ran to her as quickly as the snow would allow, which wasn't nearly fast enough. He felt as though he were trudging through a foot of wet sugar. When he reached her, it was painfully obvious that she was hurt. She'd gone pale, drained of any hint of color, as though she'd been born of the snow. His gut twisted at the sight of her.

Tears streamed down Melody's face. "I tripped and knocked her down. She made a terrible sound. I think it's her hurt foot. I'm sorry. I'm so, so sorry." She hovered around Posy, clearly wanting to do something to help, but not having any idea what might be effective.

Liam knew precisely how she felt.

"Posy." He swallowed around the lump in his throat. "What's wrong?"

"I fell." Her voice was robotic, devoid of any and all emotion, as if she were talking about someone else. Someone neither one of them knew. "I fell and twisted my foot. The injured one. It made a noise."

"A noise?" That couldn't be good.

She nodded, and it was then that he noticed the tremble in her lower lip. He could feel the tears she was trying so hard to keep inside. It was as if they were welling up in his own chest. If he closed his eyes, he could see them, as clearly as he'd seen the tears she'd shed the night of the accident. Tears he still saw when he allowed his thoughts to drift back to that night, which was something he hadn't done in years.

Until last night.

"I didn't mean to. I'm so sorry, Posy," Melody said through her sobs. She was crying in earnest now, all the tears the rest of them were holding inside.

"This isn't your fault. It was an accident, Melody. Everything is going to be fine. I promise," Liam said. He wished with everything in him that Posy had been the one to reassure her.

He told himself she was in no condition to think about the girl's feelings. There was no way she could blame anyone for what had happened. They'd been messing around.

Accidents happened. If anyone was to blame, it was him. He'd been the one in charge.

"Are you sure?" Melody blinked up at him with wide eyes.

Ronnie stepped forward and slipped an arm around her shoulders. *Interesting.* "Sure it is. Pastor will take care of Posy. Won't you, Pastor?"

Liam's own words came back to him with sickening clarity.

I'm not your keeper, Posy. Not anymore.

He pushed them away.

"Of course I will." He bent and gathered her lithe form in his arms. He placed one arm beneath her knees, the other around her back and he stood, cradling her. Even with the added bulk of her winter coat, she was featherlight. An injured bird.

"Liam, you don't need to carry me." Even as she protested, she melted into him.

He wasn't sure why he'd expected her to stiffen against his touch. She was accustomed to being carried, after all. She was a ballerina. He hadn't been the last man to wrap his arms around her. There had been others. There would be more. Men whose names Liam didn't even know. Men who would hold her, guide her movements, dance with her before hundreds of people and think nothing of the fact that in the palms of their hands rested a treasure.

"Liam," she whispered, her head falling against his shoulder. "I need to get to Anchorage. My doctor's card is in my dance bag."

He looked down as her eyes drifted closed. The tip of her nose was pink from the cold, as pink as the roses she'd always loved. Tiny crystals of snow sparkled in her eyelashes. In that moment, she was quintessentially Alaskan. The old Posy. From the looks of things, she was also in quite a bit of pain. "Don't worry about a thing. I've got you."

I've got you.

Those three words weighed more than the woman in his arms.

He fixed his gaze on Ronnie. "Get my cell phone from the office and call Zoey Wynne. Tell her I'm bringing Posy to the airport, and she needs to get to Anchorage right away."

Ronnie nodded. "Yes, sir."

"And Melody, do you know where Posy's dance bag is?" Liam asked.

"Yes." She nodded, and Liam couldn't help but notice that her tears had dried in the space of time that Ronnie had held her hand.

"Go get her doctor's business card. Meet me at the Northern Lights Inn. We need to get her on a plane. Got it?"

"Yes." She nodded again and dashed off in the direction of the church.

The next half hour passed in a blur. Once he'd gotten Posy safely tucked into Zoey's tiny plane, he could scarcely remember driving her to the airport, couldn't recall a thing he'd said to Zoey even though he was positive they'd spoken. He wasn't altogether sure which of the kids was watching his dog. It probably didn't matter. No matter who had the beast, by the end of the night there would be property damage. It was a veritable certainty.

As he stood on the frozen lake and watched Posy float into the sky toward Anchorage, he could remember only two things with absolute clarity—the weightless serenity with which she'd rested in his arms and the bittersweet kiss he'd pressed to her lips right before he shut the airplane door.

"You've got a sprain of the anterior talofibular ligament. Grade one, if you're lucky. Possibly grade two. We can't know for certain without an MRI." The doctor shrugged. "Not that it matters."

But it did matter. It mattered very much.

Posy took a deep breath and clutched the edge of the examination table. Its paper cover crinkled beneath her legs, and she heard a rip form. Just like the one in her ligament.

Grade one indicated stretching and damage to the fibers of the ligament. Grade two, on the other hand, meant at least a partial tear. When had her body become as fragile as paper?

Zoey reached for her hand and gave it a squeeze. It was funny how that squeeze seemed to be the only thing holding her together. For the time being, at least. "Why do you say it doesn't matter, Doctor?"

"It doesn't really make a difference at this point because the protocol is the same for both. We use the acronym RICE, which stands for Rest, Ice, Compression and Elevation. All things that Miss Sutton should be doing already, since she's recovering from a stress fracture." The doctor crossed his arms and eyed her as though she were one of Liam's rambunctious teenagers.

This was not good. She needed this doctor on her side. Without a note from him clearing her of any medical issues, the company wouldn't let her dance. "I am. I *am* doing those things. You have my word. I'm one hundred percent committed to getting better."

He lifted a brow. "Then explain to me again how exactly this sprain occurred."

Posy's throat went dry. "Um."

Why couldn't she force the words out?

Because you had no business romping around on crutches, throwing snowballs like a kid.

"It was just a silly accident. A snowball fight, of all things." Zoey waved a dismissive hand. "It could have happened to anyone."

But it shouldn't have happened to *her*. That was the point. She should have never placed herself—her body, which was supposed to be healing from an injury—in such a vulnerable position.

She deserved worse than a lecture from an Anchorage doctor whom she'd just met. Far worse. She deserved to be strung up by the ribbons of her pointe shoes.

A snowball fight? Really? What had she been thinking? She hadn't been thinking at all.

You were having fun. For a few unrestrained moments, you had a ball.

Her grip on the edge of the exam table tightened. Paper crumpled in her fists. She wasn't here to have fun. She was here to rest, recuperate and teach ballet. Ballet was all the fun she needed.

"I suggest you avoid any more snowball fights, at least for the time being. Understood?" The doctor reached into the pocket of his white coat and pulled out a prescription pad.

Posy nodded. "Understood."

"Do we need to come back for the MRI you mentioned?" Zoey asked.

Posy didn't know what she'd do without her. The thought of riding to and from doctors' appointments with her mother was unbearable.

The doctor shook his head. "No. That won't be necessary. Time will tell us all we need to know."

Time. The one thing that Posy didn't have.

The throbbing in her head began to rival that in her foot. She pressed her fingertips against her temples.

Zoey laid a hand on Posy's shoulder. "Are you okay? You still look awfully pale."

No. I'm about as far from okay as I can possibly get. "I'm fine. Really."

Dr. Cooper scribbled something on his pad. "I'm writing a prescription for painkillers. They'd go a long way toward making you feel more comfortable, particularly at night."

Zoey glanced at Posy. Posy's gaze dropped to her lap.

"These should help you get some sleep. I want you to remember that rest is crucial to your recovery." He ripped the page from the pad and offered it to her.

Posy stared at the square sheet of paper for several long moments before finally taking it and handing it straight to Zoey. "Thank you, Doctor."

"You're welcome. I'll see you in five days for a follow-up. I was hoping to get you out of your cast by then, but with this new hiccup, we'll just have to wait and see."

Wait and see. Wait, wait, wait. "I understand."

"Remember—RICE. Rest, Ice, Compression and Elevation. Absolutely no more snowball fights. Got it?"

"Got it."

"See you in five days. You two have a safe flight back to Aurora." He gave them a curt nod and left the room.

Just the thought of climbing back inside Zoey's airplane and flying to Aurora was exhausting. So much had happened today. Oddly enough, her injury wasn't the thing that troubled her the most. It was that kiss.

Liam had kissed her.

Right as he'd tucked her into Zoey's plane, in the final seconds before takeoff, he'd given her a look so tender that her heart had broken as surely as the bone in her foot. Then he'd touched his lips to hers.

It had been the softest of kisses, like a snowflake landing on her lips. Gentle and delicate.

But what on earth had it meant? And why was that simple kiss weighing on her mind more than her injured foot? Her foot should be her one and only concern right now.

She wished she could close her eyes and wake up the next morning in her bed back in San Francisco. No cast on her foot. No Alaska. No snowballs. No kissing her high school boyfriend.

"Ready?" Zoey asked, slipping Posy's prescription into her handbag.

Posy averted her gaze. "Let's go."

The flight home was oddly peaceful. The sun had begun to set, and the more time passed, the more Posy felt as though they were disappearing into the sky's indigo shadows. She looked down at the chunks of ice breaking away from the moody gray Alaskan shore and thought it was the perfect place to be at the moment. In between worlds. Drifting. Neither here nor there. It was the exact way she'd felt ever since she'd fallen out of her arabesque.

They traveled in silence for a while as Zoey made small adjustments to the yoke and the plane rose and fell over the misty blue tree line. Snow began to gather beneath them, and soon Posy couldn't tell whether they were moving over land or sea. Everything below was a swirl of soft white vapor, delicate and otherworldly. Like traveling through a dream.

Despite the pain in her foot, when at last Zoey broke the silence, Posy had nearly nodded off.

"So how did it go today? Other than the sprained ankle, I mean," she said.

"Awful." Posy wasn't sure she'd ever be able to listen to Prokofiev again without imagining a roomful of teen girls looking at her as if she were crazy.

"Come on. It couldn't have been that bad."

Oh, but it could. Worse, even. "It was. Trust me."

Zoey flipped a yellow switch on the plane's control panel. "How so?"

"I thought I'd be teaching little girls. I had the wrong lessons, the wrong music. I brought them *teddy bears*, for goodness sake. I had no idea they'd be teenagers. It caught me completely off guard."

Zoey turned to look at her. "You mean you came all the way here to teach ballet, and you never asked the ages of the kids?"

"Your reaction is the same as Liam's. He said the exact same thing."

Zoey's gaze returned to the view out the plane's tiny windshield. "Well, he has a point, don't you think?"

"Never mind Liam. He's the least of my problems right now." If that didn't paint a perfect picture of the sad state of affairs, nothing would.

The plane drifted on in shadowy silence until Posy felt sufficiently bathed in darkness to admit the hard truth. "They hated me."

"Who? The girls?" The tenderness in Zoey's voice was palpable. "I'm sure that's not true."

"They must. At the very best, they find me patronizing. It was terrible, Zo." An epic disaster. The cathartic act of pelting Liam with snowballs had made her forget it for a time, but as the plane crawled back to Aurora, the morning's humiliation was returning full force.

Even once she'd gotten the music straightened out and chosen something different from the playlist on her iPod, she'd still barely been able to keep their attention.

Not that she could blame them exactly. How exciting could it possibly be for a bunch of sixteen-year-olds to rise up and down on their tiptoes for the entire length of a song? Or practice sliding one foot in and out, moving from first position to second, and then back to first? Over and over again.

Relevés, pliés, the basic foot and arm positions—those were the very foundations of ballet. She couldn't start out teaching them how to leap or arabesque on day one. But that was what they'd expected, and she couldn't blame them. She'd wanted more than that at their age. Far more.

"Part of me wonders if they even believe I can dance.

They kept asking questions about my cast. It was humbling, to say the least."

Which was precisely why she'd gone outside to give Liam a piece of her mind as soon as the excruciating two-hour lesson had concluded. Although, now that she thought about it, none of it had really been his fault.

She probably should have asked Lou more questions about the job. But at the time, it had seemed less like a job offer and more like a lifeline. People didn't typically ask questions before grabbing hold of a lifeline. They generally held on as tightly as they could.

Maybe it was time to let go.

She could still go back to California. She could simply tell Lou that now that she'd further injured her foot, she didn't think teaching was such a great idea. He'd be disappointed, but she doubted the girls would mind. They'd probably even be relieved.

Somehow the prospect of going back didn't seem any more appealing than staying put.

She cleared her throat. "Thanks so much for everything you've done today, Zoey. For the ride, for staying with me at the doctor's office...all of it."

"You were hurt. I wasn't about to leave you there all alone. I can't imagine how lonely that would feel." Zoey glanced at her, then let her gaze linger when Posy grew quiet.

"Posy?"

"Yes?" She had a feeling what was coming next. She hoped she was wrong. Certain memories weren't worth revisiting, especially those that were still fresh.

"When you hurt your foot back in San Francisco, you had someone there to help you, didn't you? Please tell me you weren't alone."

Posy swallowed. "Of course not. I fell onstage, remember? There were people everywhere."

Zoey's voice went whisper-soft, barely audible above the whir of the plane's twin engine. "And afterward? At the hospital?"

"I hurt myself in the opening act. The performance had barely begun. You know...the show must go on and all that. The staff at the hospital was very accommodating." It was the truth.

So why did she feel as if she was making excuses?

"There wasn't a single person from the company who could go with you and hold your hand, tell you everything was going to be okay?"

There were all kinds of personalities in the ballet world, and while all of them were excellent at creating beauty through dance, Posy didn't know many who were adept at hand holding. "It was an important show. Opening night."

The air in the small plane was thick with disappointment. Posy wasn't altogether sure if it was hers or Zoey's.

"The company sent me a beautiful flower arrangement the next day, though. Pink roses. Very pretty."

This news cheered Zoey, as Posy knew it would. "Roses. Now, there's a treat I haven't seen in a while."

Since she'd first slipped on a pair of ballet shoes, Posy's dreams had been rose-scented. While roses of all colors and varieties were commonplace at nearly every supermarket florist in the Lower 48, they were a rarity in Alaska. Pretty much the only way to procure a bouquet of roses in Aurora was to fly them in from Anchorage or, more often, Seattle. The long-stemmed beauties were as priceless as the gold dust that hopeful tourists still sought on panning tours down at Resurrection Creek on the Kenai Peninsula.

Posy could still remember the first time she'd seen a photograph of a ballerina bent into a deep curtsy at the end of a performance. The stage had been littered with red roses. A crimson carpet. The ballerina had worn a glittering tiara and held an ample bouquet in her willowy arms.

Two or three dozen flowers at least. To a little girl from Alaska who'd never inhaled the perfume of a real rosebud, it had been the most extravagant of riches imaginable.

That had been years ago. Since then, Posy had been presented with more roses than she could count. But it never lost its charm. She was certain it never would.

"We're just about to the airstrip, but first I have something special to show you." Zoey maneuvered the plane into a sweeping curve. "Take a look down below."

Posy squinted into the darkness beyond the airplane windows. Snowflakes danced against the glass in a silent, moonlit ballet. She couldn't see a thing beyond the inky-black evergreens. She leaned closer and pressed her hand against the window. It was cold to the touch, and her breath landed on it in a soft, gray fog. Just when she was about to give up, she spotted movement among the shadows. She looked closer and made out a shape. Then another. And another.

Reindeer.

They were leaping and playing in the snow. An entire herd, their movements so graceful that it almost looked as though they were dancing.

Dasher...Prancer...

Dancer.

"They're gorgeous." A lump formed in Posy's throat. She couldn't believe it. She was getting emotional over a bunch of reindeer. It wasn't as if she'd never seen one before. She'd grown up around them.

But she'd never seen them like this before. Dancing with abandon. The way they moved together was remarkable, almost as though it had been choreographed. The fact that it hadn't, that it was spontaneous and natural, made it all the more special.

Something stirred in Posy's soul. Something she hadn't felt in a very long time and couldn't quite name.

"Don't tell me this is your farm." She couldn't imagine witnessing such a glorious display every night. "Are they yours?"

Zoey grinned. "Every last one."

"How many are there?"

"Thirty-one." She grimaced. "Sometimes thirty. One of them is somewhat of a delinquent and runs away on occasion."

Runaway reindeer. She was definitely back in Alaska.

Chapter Nine

The ground grew closer and closer until the plane finally touched down on the mirrored ice surface of the frozen lake that served as Aurora's airport runway.

"Home sweet home." Zoey taxied to the far end of the lake and brought the plane to a stop. "Wait right here. I don't want you trying to walk on the ice. I think there's a wheelchair in the office."

"Okay." Posy wasn't about to argue with her. As much as she loathed the idea of exiting the runway in a wheelchair, Dr. Cooper's lecture still rang in her ears.

Rest, Ice, Compression, Elevation.

Somehow, crossing an ice-covered body of water on crutches didn't seem to fit anywhere on that list.

She pulled on her mittens and waited in the silent cockpit. Snow fell from the sky thicker than it had all day. She could no longer see a thing out the window. Just a dizzying swirl of snowflakes. When at last someone rapped on the window, she jumped.

She opened the door. "You scared me, Zoey."

But it wasn't Zoey.

Liam stood outside the plane, and there wasn't a wheelchair in sight. "Hi."

What was he doing here? Surely he hadn't been waiting around this entire time. "Hi."

"I came out to give you a hand. The wheelchair has gone missing. If I had to venture a guess, I'd say someone is using it to haul firewood again." He shrugged. "I guess there's typically not much use for it otherwise."

"Oh. Okay, well…" Before she could gather her crutches and swing her legs out of the plane, Liam scooped her up in his arms.

She hadn't expected it this time. "Again?" she asked, anchoring her arms around his neck because, really, what else was she supposed to do with them?

"Again." He gave her a tight smile. "Humor me, would you? The last time I saw you, I was worried I'd ruined you permanently."

Wait. What?

"This wasn't your fault." She willed her body to relax in his arms. *Don't make this a bigger deal than it is. He's simply trying to help.*

How often had she been carried by male dancers, bodies pressed tightly against one another, and thought nothing of it? Countless times. Every day. For years.

But this was different. It felt intimate. It shouldn't, but it did.

They were alone on the ice, wrapped in darkness and starlight. In the darkness of the evening shadows, the rest of Posy's senses were heightened. The crunch of Liam's hiking boots against the ice seemed impossibly loud. He had that woodsy smell that she'd noticed the last time he'd carried her. Damp earth and pine needles. She had to stop herself from burrowing her head into his shoulder and letting her eyes drift closed.

She was tired. That was all. It had been a long day. The longest.

And she couldn't stop thinking about the kiss.

"I was in charge of things at the church, and you got hurt." Liam's words rumbled angrily in his chest. "I'm responsible."

"I'm the one who went marching into the snow. And as I recall, I threw the first snowball. You said you weren't my keeper. Remember?"

He shook his head. "That was before I realized just how much you need looking after."

The lingering sweetness of the kiss began to sour. "I don't need looking after. I'm perfectly capable of taking care of myself."

"Because it's late and you gave me such a scare earlier, I'm going to be nice and refrain from pointing out that you're being carried at the moment." He pinned her with a look. "By necessity."

She wanted to scream for him to put her down. And she would have, if not for the fact that he was right. It was sort of necessary. "Thank you," she muttered.

"It's nothing. I'd do the same for any of the kids."

An icy stab of disappointment hit her square in the chest.

I'd do the same for any of the kids.

Was that how he saw her? As that same messed-up teen girl she'd been so long ago?

She didn't want him to think of her as his responsibility. As someone to look after, like one of the kids.

What difference does it make? Until a few days ago, it hadn't mattered if he'd thought of you at all.

Liam pushed through the back door of the Northern Lights Inn with Posy in his arms so quietly that at first their entrance went unnoticed. Their presence was pretty much lost in the hum of activity and the chattering of teenagers accompanied by the strum of Caleb's guitar.

Every member of the church youth group was there,

as they had been all night awaiting Posy's return. Every boy and every girl. They huddled on the oversize leather sofas facing the fireplace. Empty cups from the coffee bar littered the coffee table.

"What's this?" Posy asked. "Surely all of them haven't been here the entire time."

Liam looked down and realized she was still in his arms.

Put her down, you idiot.

She angled her face toward his to look at him, and for the briefest of moments, their eyes met. All Liam could think about was the kiss. That kiss that had come from nowhere.

He wished he could take it back. He would have gotten down on his knees and prayed for time to move backward so he could undo it if he thought such a prayer would be granted. To unkiss Posy.

He'd been worried about her. That was all. He shouldn't have been. She'd be dancing in no time. Even if both of her feet somehow fell right off, she'd still somehow end up dancing off into the sunset.

Posy's gaze fixed with his, and he realized he'd still had yet to set her on her feet. Her face was so close to his that he could see the tiny gold flecks in her gray eyes. Hidden treasure. "You shouldn't have made them stay, Liam. Not for me."

"Are you kidding? This wasn't my idea. You know how I feel about airports." He lowered her to the ground, waited to make sure she was steady on her feet and then released his hold on her.

His hands felt oddly empty all of a sudden.

"Then what's going on? It looks like the entire youth group is here." She shook her head. "Including your nutty dog. Really, Liam? The dog, too?"

He decided to ignore the dog comment. "The kids are

here because they wanted to stay. They were worried about you. I repeat—it wasn't my idea."

"Yet here you are." She aimed her gaze out the window at a ski plane taking off in the darkness and then back at him. "At an airport."

She had a point. What exactly was he doing here?

"I couldn't very well leave the kids unsupervised." As if it was his job to watch them twenty-four hours a day.

"Right."

"Don't read into it." But she was. He could tell. She had that look about her that she always had when she was concentrating on something very hard. Brow slightly furrowed, lips pressed together.

Only this time she was smiling. "It's nice."

Liam shoved his hands in his pockets and considered that possibly he needed to take his own advice. *Don't read into it.* "The girls have been watching YouTube videos of you on my iPad all night long. You'd better prepare yourself for tomorrow."

"Tomorrow?" There was a hint of bewilderment in her tone. "I sort of thought I was finished at the church."

"Finished? After one day?"

"They didn't seem all that interested."

"They're teenagers. They never seem interested. Give it time." He couldn't believe the words that were coming out of his mouth. She was on the verge of forgetting the whole ballet thing. That was what he wanted, wasn't it? Why the pep talk?

"I don't know. I'm not sure what I can teach teenagers in such a short time, or if they even really want to learn. Sometimes I think…"

Whatever she said next was drowned out by the ear-splitting squeals of the girls when they realized Posy had finally reappeared. They surrounded her, peppering her with questions and well-wishes.

"You're back!"

"Posy!"

"Ohmygosh, is your foot okay?"

Even the boys gathered around, although Liam had noticed that Ronnie had been avoiding Melody like the plague once again. And there had been one or two wadded-up napkins thrown in her general direction over the course of the evening.

"Kids, settle down. Let's give Posy some space, okay?" Liam could just see them toppling her over and injuring her further. His head hurt with the possibility.

"It's fine," Posy said. "Really."

She was smiling wider than Liam had seen her smile since her return to Alaska, which didn't make a whole lot of sense. It was pretty obvious by the hesitancy of her movements that she was in pain. He was certain she was thinking about her dancing. Worrying about it. Dance was always first and foremost on her mind.

"Posy, we saw you dance on the internet. It was amazing," Melody said.

"Thank you." Posy's cheeks glowed pink. "Which ballet did you see?"

"You were wearing a white tutu," Ava said. The tutu seemed to have made an impression on all the girls.

"Ah, that must have been *Swan Lake*." Then she launched into a story about how it had been her first performance with the company.

Liam stepped back so she could give the girls her full attention. He didn't need to hear the story anyway. He'd known *Swan Lake* had been her first real ballet, although he'd never been able to bring himself to watch the video. That had been in the weeks when the aftermath of Posy's accident, of her leaving, had been the most painful. Like an open wound stubborn to heal. Why would he have tortured himself in such a way?

He sank onto one of the bar stools at the coffee counter. Then a gust of frigid wind blew inside as Zoey walked through the door.

She stomped the snow off her feet, removed the shabby flannel hat she always seemed to wear and sidled up alongside Liam. "I finally got the plane all tucked away for the night. I didn't know I was missing out on a party. Wow, look at this. You guys stayed here and waited all evening to see how Posy was doing?"

"The kids were worried about her." Liam cleared his throat.

"The kids. Sure." Zoey smirked.

Liam narrowed his gaze at her. "Really. The kids. She gave them a genuine scare earlier. Can't you tell how glad they are to see her?"

"I can, actually. And you have no idea how happy it makes me to see you all here to welcome her back. It means more to her than you know."

He shook his head. "It's nothing."

"It's not nothing. It's something." Zoey lowered her voice. "She needs this, Liam. She does."

Liam glanced at her and saw concern in her gaze. He didn't like it. Not at all. "What aren't you telling me?"

"It's just a hunch, but I don't think her life in California is quite as wonderful as she lets on. I think the real reason she's here is because without dance, she doesn't have a life there."

Without dance. Those were the key words in her sentence. "She's planning on dancing again, though. You know that."

"Yes, but..." She glanced at Posy, then back at him. "I saw the kiss, Liam."

Great. Now not only did he have to accept the fact that he couldn't undo it, but he was also being forced to talk about it. "Zoey, please."

She shrugged. "I was right there, you know. I couldn't help but notice."

"Well, try and forget it, okay?"

She lifted a brow. "Is that what you're doing? Trying to forget?"

He looked at her for a long, loaded moment. "It seems I'm always trying to forget."

"She's back now, though. Surely that means something."

"I told you. It means she can't dance. It won't last forever. She'll be on the first plane out of here once she's better."

Zoey aimed her gaze across the room at Posy. "Do you really think so?"

There was no doubt in his mind. None whatsoever. "Mark my words. The clock is ticking."

Chapter Ten

"Are you sure you should be teaching?" Posy's mother hovered at the foot of the sofa where Posy was stretched out, elevating and icing her foot before she had to leave for church. She'd been doing that an awful lot. Hovering. "You're hurt."

Posy adjusted the position of her ice pack. "I was hurt when I got here. Remember? That's why I came back in the first place."

"Not this hurt." Her mother frowned. She'd been doing an awful lot of that, too.

"I'm fine. It's a sprained ankle. Dancers sprain their ankles all the time." Granted, they didn't sprain them in snowball fights, and not when they already had broken bones. But it would be okay. It would. She'd been following Dr. Cooper's protocol to the letter. Rest, ice, compression, elevation. She was pretty sure she'd been murmuring those words in her sleep.

It would be okay. It had to.

"I still think it would be a good idea if you just stayed home. I'm sure Liam would understand."

"This isn't about Liam, Mom. It's about the girls in the

youth group. I don't want to let them down." Not to mention the fact that she'd go crazy if she stayed here all day.

A blast of winter wind blew through the living room, and the front door slammed. Posy's dad walked in, shaking his head. "Well, honey. It looks like your rental car has a flat tire."

"What?" Posy sighed.

Come on, God. I know there are people out there with way bigger problems than mine, but I'm ready for something to go my way. Anything.

"Oh, dear. I guess that means you're stuck here," her mom said. No doubt she was dancing a jig inside.

"No." Posy shook her head. "I can't be stuck here. I have a job."

There was no way she could stay here all day with her mom watching her like a hawk. Not when the kids had waited all night for her to come back from Anchorage.

She pushed herself off the sofa and stood, albeit awkwardly. "I'll just call a cab."

"Nonsense. Take my car." Her dad reached in his pocket and held out his keys.

"Hank." Her mother gave a nearly imperceptible shake of her head. But Posy saw it.

So did her father, but he promptly ignored it. "You don't need to be driving around in a rental car anyway. Not when we have two perfectly good automobiles sitting in the driveway."

"It's okay. Really, it is. I can call a cab and get the rental-car company to come fix the flat." Posy grabbed her dance bag, slung it over her shoulder and reached for her crutches.

There was a world of silent communication going on between her parents. It made her stomach hurt to witness it.

She'd known the car situation would be awkward, which

was why she'd rented one to begin with, even though it would surely break the bank. The last time she'd driven one of her parents' cars, she'd wrapped it around a tree. And it had been all her fault. Could she blame her mom for worrying? Not really.

"Posy, here. Take the keys." Her father jingled his key ring.

Posy glanced at her mom, who was busy staring at the floor. "Are you sure?"

"Yes, I'm sure. Here. Take them." He smiled.

Posy didn't think she'd ever loved him more than she did at that moment. "Thanks, Dad."

She took the keys, wishing there was something she could do or say to alleviate some of the tension in the room—offer to let her mom go through her dance bag? There was nothing there. She'd never even filled Dr. Cooper's prescription. As far as she knew, it was still buried in Zoey's purse.

A search and seizure wasn't the answer anyway. She was just going to have to prove to people she could be trusted again. Her dad. Her mom.

Liam.

Why did her thoughts keep going back to him, time and time again?

Her cell phone rang, and she was grateful to have something else to occupy her mind. Until she fished her phone from her dance bag and saw the name of the caller on the display screen.

Gabriel. The director of the ballet company.

A wave of panic washed over her. Why was Gabriel calling?

Calm down. He's probably just checking on your injury.

Right. And just what was she supposed to tell him? She turned the ringer off and shoved her phone back in her bag.

"Aren't you going to get that?" her dad asked.

She shook her head. "It can wait."

Could it? Could it really?

"I close the pond for one night and this happens." Liam crossed his arms and stared at the reindeer in the middle of the ice. The animal had been lying there with his legs tucked beneath him when Liam had driven by just to check on things on the way to church, and an hour later he was still there.

Fortunately, there was only one reindeer in town notorious for getting in trouble. And Liam knew his name, as did pretty much everyone in a fifty-mile radius of Aurora.

"Palmer," Alec muttered. He'd come straight over when Liam called with news of the reindeer sit-in.

"That's him, isn't it?" Liam said.

"Of course it's him." Alec rolled his eyes. "It's always him."

He might sound exasperated, but Liam knew Palmer was Alec's favorite reindeer on the farm he shared with Zoey. He had a soft spot for the animal in spite of his mischievous streak. Maybe because of it.

They stood on the snowy edge of the pond, watching... waiting. Alec sighed. Liam sighed. Even Sundog sighed.

Finally Liam asked, "What are the odds we can get him to move before tonight? Or should I just tell everyone to skate circles around him?"

"I can get him up. I was just sort of hoping he'd see me and decide to amble on over here." He pulled a handful of carrots from his pocket.

Sundog stood, tail swinging back and forth like a pendulum. Alec tossed him a carrot.

"Every time I see your dog, he's either eating something or planning his next meal. Snow. Carrots. Buckets." He aimed a bemused glance at a shredded red bucket half buried in the snow beside the snack bar. Sundog's latest casualty. "Do you ever feed him?"

Liam lifted a brow. "Come on. Sundog isn't all that bad. Besides, people with runaway reindeer shouldn't throw stones."

"Point taken." Alec shrugged. "Hey, I've been meaning to ask you. How did you come up with the name Sundog anyway?"

Liam grew very still. "Why?"

"No reason. I just like it, that's all. It's different," Alec said.

He kept his gaze firmly fixed on the dog. "It just came to me, I guess. No particular reason."

"Give me a hand with the beast?"

"Sure."

They walked across the pond, stepping gingerly on the ice. Palmer didn't move a muscle, even when they got within three feet of him. He snored so loud that Liam wondered if the ice might crack.

Alec rested a hand on the reindeer's head. "Hey, bud. It's time to go home."

Palmer woke with a snort.

Alec backed up and held out his hand with a carrot resting in the center of his palm. The reindeer scrambled to his feet.

"Here." Alec tossed Liam a rope.

Liam looped it over Palmer's massive head while he munched on carrots. A leash of sorts. Now that Liam thought about it, the reindeer wasn't all that much bigger than Sundog.

Liam handed Alec the rope, and they began a slow, careful walk off the ice.

"So the pond was closed last night, huh?" Alec said over the sound of Palmer crunching on a carrot and Sundog barking with envy from the sidelines.

"Yeah. I was at the Northern Lights Inn with the kids. They were waiting for Posy and Zoey, and I didn't want to leave them there alone." As if they were five-year-olds instead of teenagers who had jobs and would be going off to college soon.

"Right," Alec said, the single syllable carrying more weight than it should have.

Liam sighed. "You've been talking to your wife, haven't you?"

Palmer gave Alec a nudge with his muzzle, and Alec offered him another carrot that was quickly gobbled up. "We tend to do that on occasion. Talk to one another."

Funny. Very funny. "Look. I don't know what she told you, but…"

"Actually, she told me that Posy didn't want the prescription for pain pills that the doctor gave her," Alec said quietly. "In case you were interested."

"I'm not." Liam's response was automatic, even if the tug of longing brought about by Alec's words was anything but ordinary.

"Fair enough."

There was a beat of silence and then Liam heard himself ask, "Did he give them to her anyway? The pain pills?"

What was he doing? He'd promised himself he wouldn't get involved.

"He wrote her a prescription," Alec said.

Unease settled in Liam's gut.

"Which she gave to Zoey," he added. The knot in the pit of Liam's stomach unwound ever so slightly. "She tore it up when she got home. It's in our trash can right now in tatters."

Liam said nothing. As much relief as this information brought, it felt wrong being privy to it. As if he were spying on Posy.

"Look," Alec said after a long silence, "I just thought you'd want to know."

"Thanks, but it's really none of my business." Liam stepped off the ice and onto the snowy bank of the pond.

Alec followed suit, with Palmer now walking obediently alongside him. Even the town's naughtiest reindeer could be better behaved than Sundog. Super.

"You sure about that?"

Yes. "Mostly."

"One more thing…"

Liam sighed. He knew it would come around to this. Did married people have to talk about *everything*? He threw up his hands. "Yes, I kissed her. All right? It was a mistake—one I don't intend on repeating. But I did it. I kissed her right there in front of Zoey. Satisfied?"

Alec frowned. "No, actually. She didn't tell me that part."

"Really?" Liam watched as Sundog gave Palmer a wary sniff. The dog seemed taken aback to meet a creature taller than himself.

Palmer snorted. Sundog leaped backward and hid behind Liam's legs.

"Really." There was a distinct note of bewilderment in Alec's tone. Apparently there were a few things married people managed to keep to themselves.

"Oh." Liam gave Sundog a reassuring pat on the head. "Do me a favor and forget I told you. I'm doing my best to forget about it myself."

Alec laughed. "Good luck with that."

"Your commentary isn't helping." Liam slid him a sideways glance.

"Sorry."

A change of subject was in order. Pronto. "So what is it, then? The one last thing you wanted to tell me?"

"Oh, right. Zoey has a flight scheduled up to Kivalina

in a few weeks. She has a load of medical supplies to drop off. Your parents are up there, aren't they?"

Liam nodded. He knew what was coming, and it was the one topic he wished to discuss even less than the kiss he'd given Posy.

"Zoey says you're welcome to tag along if you'd like to visit your folks."

"I don't think so. Between the youth group and the skating rink, my plate is pretty full."

Alec nodded and was kind enough not to remind Liam that he'd just closed the pond the night before. "I understand. Believe me, I do. She just asked me to pass along the offer."

Liam pasted on a smile. "Tell her I said thanks."

"Will do." Alec stroked Palmer's head in the round, flat space between his antlers. "And I appreciate the help with Palmer."

"No problem. Have you and Zoey figured out why he keeps getting out?"

"No. It's a mystery." Alec gave Palmer a long, thoughtful look. "He's got everything he could ever want or need back home. He's happy there. He's loved. I suppose that no matter the circumstances, there will always be certain souls who want to wander. The restless ones."

"I guess you're right," Liam said.

The ache that had hit him when Alec first mentioned Posy returned with gnawing intensity.

There will always be certain souls who want to wander. The restless ones.

Maybe Alec was right. Maybe it couldn't be helped.

But what about the others? The ones the restless souls left behind, aching in their wake?

What about them?

The numbness afforded by Posy's ice pack began to wear off faster than Posy could back her father's car out of the driveway. By the time she reached the stop sign at the end of the block, her foot was throbbing again.

Ever so briefly, she thought about the prescription that Dr. Cooper had written for her the night before. She closed her eyes and heard the scratch of his pen as it moved across the paper.

No. I can't. I won't.

What was more, she didn't want to. Not really. She needed to feel everything that was going on in her body. The pain was her teacher. If she paid attention to it, she would know when she was overdoing it and needed to rest. She needed to listen to her body instead of muting it like before.

She'd learned that much. As much as she didn't like dwelling on the past, there were parts of it that clung to her. Memories forged. Lessons learned.

If she didn't let herself feel, she risked hurting herself so badly that she would never recover, never dance again.

Let myself feel. She gripped the steering wheel and lifted her gaze to the lapis-blue sky. *Why is that so hard to do?*

She squared her shoulders and guided the car in the direction of the church. It would pass, this explosion of sensation. Everything in Alaska seemed bigger, brighter, more intense than it did anywhere else. But that was normal, right? It was only natural to feel a bit sentimental now that she was back home.

Everything would be fine.

She'd just about convinced herself that was the case when she guided the car around the next corner and found herself driving beneath the graceful blue branches of a majestic tree.

The tree.

She slowed to a stop, as if she could somehow prevent the onslaught of memories from rushing forward. The darkness, the rain, the way everything had looked so surreal and blurry around the edges. The squeal of the tires. The sickening jolt of the impact when she'd slammed into the centuries-old tree trunk. How even then she still hadn't been coherent enough to process what was happening. None of it had seemed real until she'd seen the wreckage reflected in the sorrow of Liam's eyes.

In the here and now, a terrible ache blossomed in her chest. She had trouble catching her breath. Every gulp of air seemed inadequate.

She pulled over to the side of the road and rested her forehead on the steering wheel.

Breathe, Posy. Just breathe. It was a long time ago.

Then why did the memory feel so fresh? Raw. As if it had just happened yesterday.

Probably because she hadn't been back here since that awful night. Even before she'd left Aurora, in those final weeks after everything had come to humiliating light, she'd steadfastly avoided this route. When her mother had driven her to and from her doctor's appointments, she'd gone the long way around the center of town. They'd never discussed the fact that Posy could no longer bear to look at the tree. It had simply been an unspoken understanding between them.

Then Posy had left and carried her final memory of the tree—rain-soaked and silvery and beautiful, even in the wreckage—away with her.

She couldn't believe she'd made the mistake of driving past it now. She'd been preoccupied with the discomfort in her foot as well as the excitement she'd felt at starting over with the girls at the church. Her mind had been spinning in dizzying pirouettes.

It's a tree, not a memory. That's all. Just a tree.

She forced herself to look at it. Really look at it, in all of its cerulean glory, sunlight shooting in sparks from its slender blue needles. Posy wasn't sure what she'd expected. A gaping hole, maybe? A telltale dent in its bark? Some sort of sign of what had happened there so long ago. But there was nothing. The only scars from that night belonged to her.

And Liam.

Tears filled her eyes, and the tree grew blurry, like a watercolor painting.

Stop. It's just a tree.

But it had never been just a tree, had it?

Long before the accident, this had been their special place. Hers and Liam's. Beneath these branches, he'd asked her out for the first time. It had been the scene of their first picnic and the first time Liam had held her hand. It had witnessed their first kiss.

Posy brushed her fingertips along her lips and let herself remember the smell of pine and the way the snow had danced so lightly on her skin as he'd angled his face toward hers. She'd closed her eyes, unsure what to expect. She'd never been kissed before, by Liam or any other boy. She'd been so nervous, but not in a fearful way. Sweet anticipation had coiled in her belly, much in the way it did in the moments immediately before she launched herself into a grand jeté at ballet class.

The kiss had taken her by surprise in the quietest of ways, like an unexpected summer snowfall. It had been a reverent kiss, a whisper of a touch. Liam's gentle grace had left her breathless, and when she'd opened her eyes, every strange, new emotion she'd been experiencing had somehow been painted on the sky.

She'd heard of the expression "seeing stars" before. But when Liam Blake kissed Posy the very first time, she'd seen three suns. Three suns surrounded by a blinding circle of colorful light. Arching lavender and tangerine streaks exploding against the glacier-blue horizon, connected by a ring of sunshine and those three glowing golden stars.

"Liam, look," she'd whispered, fearful of talking too loudly and interrupting nature's spectacular dance.

The look on his face as he'd turned his gaze to the sky had been lovelier, more luminous than a thousand suns. "What's happening?"

"It's the sun setting, combined with the cold. It happens here sometimes, when there are ice crystals in the air. Sort of like an Alaskan rainbow. You mean you've never seen one before?"

Liam had still been new to Aurora, but he'd told her all about moving from place to place and how his father preached in the most remote villages in the Arctic Circle. Surely he'd seen more and done more than she could have ever imagined.

But he'd never seen anything like the sky that day. "No, never. What is its name?"

He'd pulled her closer, and beneath the moody blue shelter of their tree, she'd burrowed into Liam's embrace. Neither of them had been quite ready to look away from the sun. Even seven years later, Posy could remember hoping that if she'd just kept her eyes on the blinding light, she would always feel as she did at that precise moment. Treasured.

That had been the moment she'd known she'd fallen in love.

With a lump in her throat and a heart aching with tenderness, she'd answered Liam's question. "They call it a sun dog."

Chapter Eleven

"Liam, a word, please?" Pastor McNeil stuck his head out the church door and motioned for Liam to come inside.

"Certainly. I'll be right there." He finished packing the snowball cradled in his hands and added it to the pile he'd been working on all morning.

Eight hundred fifty-six down.

One hundred forty-four to go.

He glanced at his watch. He still had several hours until school got out. No problem, assuming that whatever his boss wanted to discuss wouldn't take the better part of the afternoon. He couldn't imagine it would. Then again, he wasn't typically summoned to the head pastor's office. He actually didn't spend much time in meetings with Lou at all. The fact that this was the second time in as many weeks that he'd be sitting across that great expanse of desk wasn't without significance.

He brushed the snow from his gloves and headed inside. The blast of warm air was such a sea change from the temperature outdoors that for a moment, he was disoriented. He blinked against the assault of central heating. With pinpricks of pain, his face dethawed. By the time he reached Pastor McNeil's office, he could once again feel his mouth. His ears, fingers and toes were still a different story.

He pulled off his gloves and knocked on the open door. "You need something, Pastor?"

Lou looked up and waved him inside. "Come in. Have a seat."

"Yes, sir." Liam shed his parka and sat.

"That's quite a stack of snowballs you've got out there."

"Yes, it is. I'm almost finished. In a regulation snowball fight, the team is allowed one thousand snowballs. The past few days, we've been using half of our practice time making our ammunition, so I thought I'd get a head start today. I want the boys to get a feel for just how quickly they can go through that many snowballs." Liam was guessing it would be far quicker than they expected.

"And your first official game is coming up soon, isn't it?"

"Yes, sir. This weekend. I know the boys would be thrilled if you could come cheer them on."

"I wouldn't miss it. I suppose Josephine will be there with the girls, as well?"

The use of Posy's stage name caught Liam off guard again. Why did it seem to grate on his nerves more and more every time he heard it? She'd been back for nearly three weeks now. He'd heard the name tossed about practically every day. *Josephine Sutton.* Some of the girls had even taken to calling her Miss Josephine. She'd asked them to call her Posy, but the discovery of her YouTube videos had kindled their interest in her stage name. They were suddenly fascinated with all sorts of new things, each and every one of which was in some way related to ballet.

"I don't know, sir. We haven't discussed it." Pastor Mc-Neil frowned to such an extent that Liam added a hasty "*Yet.* We haven't discussed it *yet.*"

"I certainly hope that's on your agenda for this afternoon. The game is in two days, is it not? I know you want every member of the youth group there." Liam's boss peered over the top of his glasses.

He had a valid point. The boys would get a huge kick out of the girls watching their game. Besides, Liam had never split the group before. The entire idea of the boys and girls doing different things was somewhat of a novelty, and never would have happened without that fateful snowball Ronnie had aimed at Melody's head. "Of course. Yes. I'll make sure Miss Sutton gets it on her schedule." He still couldn't call her Josephine. No way.

"How are things working out with Josephine's ballet lessons? It's been a few weeks, so I wanted to touch base with you." Pastor McNeil's brow furrowed in the way it always did when he was serious about something, and Liam knew that this was the moment he could raise an objection about the girls and ballet.

Posy wasn't around. It was just him and Lou. And Sundog, of course. But this was the one instance that Liam knew the dog wouldn't be a problem unless, unbeknownst to him, the Newfoundland had learned to talk. Which he really doubted, since he'd yet to learn to stop chewing on the furniture.

Liam released a tense breath. He couldn't do it. It didn't feel right. "Actually, the girls seem really happy."

"Is that right?"

"Yes." He nodded.

Ballet fever had struck the youth group. Since the vigil the night that Posy had sprained her ankle, the girls had become more and more enamored with her. Every afternoon, they held on to the backs of their metal chairs and rose up on their sock feet, faces aglow as if they were dancing in one of the fancy productions on Posy's YouTube videos.

He still had the nagging fear that one of them would get hurt, but that seemed unlikely since they appeared to be doing the most basic of ballet moves. Posy would be long gone before they were ready to leap or be lifted in the air. She would leave as surely as the snow would fall.

And this time when she was gone, he wouldn't be the one left nursing a hole in his heart. This time it would be worse. Seven teenage girls would be left floundering in her wake. It was a helpless inevitability. He couldn't stop it from happening if he tried.

"I'm glad to hear that." Lou nodded. Then, just when Liam thought the discussion was over, he dropped the bomb. "Because I'd like you to talk to Josephine about putting together a dance recital."

"What?" It came out far louder than he'd planned. Sundog even jerked his head up and let out a woof of protest.

"Is that a problem?"

"Well, sir. They've only taken a dozen lessons or so, and Miss Sutton will be gone in a matter of weeks."

"Perfect timing, then." Pastor McNeil reached inside his desk drawer, removed a single sheet of paper and slid it across the desk toward Liam.

Liam glanced at the words at the top of the bright yellow page. *State Grant to be Awarded for Youth Program. Deadline to Apply: April 1.*

Liam slid the paper back toward his boss. He didn't need to read it in its entirety. He already had a copy of it on the desk in his office.

"I don't understand." Liam shook his head. "What does this have to do with a ballet recital?"

"The state of Alaska is awarding a grant to a youth program that brings something unique to the state and its community. There's government money to be had. The kind of money that could really make a difference in the lives of the kids here."

He wasn't saying anything Liam didn't know already. "Yes, I'm aware. I'm already planning to apply for the grant. I've been waiting until the boys' first snowballing match. I'm going to take photos and a video to attach to the form."

"Forgive me, Liam. But I fail to see how Alaskan kids throwing snowballs is going to seem unique in any way. We need something that sets our program apart. Something the other youth programs in the state don't have." He leaned back in his chair and waited for Liam to agree with him.

He'd given voice to Liam's overriding concern. Snow and Alaska weren't exactly an unexpected combination. "And you think Posy's ballet classes are deserving of this grant? Classes that she's been teaching for such a short time?"

Lou shook his head. "No, I don't."

Good. They were in agreement.

"But if she can put together a dance recital, I think we have a real chance. Think about it, Liam. A dance recital. Organized by a professional ballerina. Name one youth program that can make that claim."

He had a point. "I can't. Ours included."

Pastor McNeil shrugged. "But surely it could be done."

What in the world had Posy said to this man to make him think she could turn anyone into a ballerina overnight?

"Pastor, these girls are only learning the basics. The deadline to apply for this grant is in three weeks. I just don't think having them ready for a dance recital by then is in the realm of possibility." Liam had dropped in on Posy's classes. The girls were wobbly even when holding on to the backs of their chairs.

And even if Posy somehow managed to pull it off, wouldn't a recital just intensify things? The girls were already growing attached to Posy. Too attached. They needed distance and space, before it was forced upon them by her absence. What Lou was suggesting would be the very opposite of distance.

Pastor McNeil drummed his fingertips on his desk. "I believe that is a decision for Josephine. Don't you agree?"

What was Liam supposed to say to that?

"Shall you talk to her, or shall I?" Lou stood, ready to sprint down the hall in search of Posy.

Sundog rose to his feet, ready to sprint after him. The dog had taken to hanging around Posy whenever Liam turned his back. Was there anyone in Alaska who'd yet to become enamored with her?

"I'll do it." Liam suppressed a sigh. "I'll talk to her."

A recital.

If she could put a show together, their chances of winning the grant would improve exponentially. Ballet wasn't exactly commonplace in Alaska. And Liam wanted that grant. The church needed it. The kids needed it.

But in three weeks' time? Impossible.

"A recital?" Posy stared at Liam, searching his expression for a sign, *any* sign, that he was joking. "You're serious?"

"Yes." He crossed his arms. "Not me, technically. Lou."

Well, that made more sense. But it didn't change the fact that, for all their newfound enthusiasm, the girls were still very much beginners.

They'd barely moved beyond the basic plié. But had any dancer in the history of ballet ever moved beyond the plié? As Balanchine's legendary muse Suzanne Farrell once said, *Plié is the first thing you learn and the last thing you master.*

She adjusted the bag of ice on her foot. Her toes had gone numb, and she had no idea if the coolness was even penetrating her cast, but she wasn't taking chances. She had an appointment with Dr. Cooper first thing in the morning, and she wanted to be able to look him in the eye and tell him that she'd been a model patient.

"Assuming I could choreograph something basic—and we're talking *very* basic…" But basic could still be graceful. There was something innately pure and beautiful in the simplicity of a pointed toe, a delicately arched arm. Breathtaking innocence. "A recital would mean costumes. Dance clothes instead of sweatpants and T-shirts. Real ballet shoes instead of sock feet."

"The church doesn't have the money for those things, Posy. Especially for a program with an expiration date." He gave her a meaningful glance. She looked back down at the bag of ice on her leg. "Lou asked me to talk to you about it, and I said that I would. For the record, I told him it was impossible."

"I said there were difficulties involved. I never said it was impossible." Just *near* impossible. Still too far out of the realm of possibility to even contemplate.

Yet the image of the girls in pink shoes and soft, romantic tutus had already begun tiptoeing in her head.

They would love it. She was sure they would. Getting all dressed up and showing off the new ballet skills they'd learned would put the biggest smiles on their faces. It would be exactly the kind of confidence that kids that age needed most. Most of all, it would be fun. And what better parting gift for her to leave them when she went back to her real life?

Real life.

The phrase settled in the pit of her stomach. The longer she stayed in Alaska, the blurrier the line between *real* and *not real* seemed to get.

"Posy." Liam sighed. "I can't get you a dime for costumes and shoes. Or anything else. I wish I could. For the girls' sake, of course."

For the girls. Naturally. That was why they were both

here, having this discussion. That was why she spent the majority of her waking hours with Liam. For the kids.

Somewhere up above, she sensed God rolling His eyes.

She cleared her throat. Then just as she was about to ask her next question, her cell phone blared to life. The familiar, dramatic notes of Tchaikovsky filled the air, albeit slightly tinnier than they'd sounded coming from the orchestra pit in the theater where she danced.

Liam promptly rolled his eyes. "Nice ringtone."

"I think so." She gave him a saccharine smile and reached for her phone. But her smile faded when she saw the name on the display.

Gabriel.

Again.

She'd been dodging his calls for two weeks now. She just couldn't seem to make herself pick up the phone and talk to him. Not until her cast was off, when she could tell him with complete honesty that she was almost healed.

One more day. Just one more day.

God, please.

She silenced the ringtone and buried her phone back in her dance bag.

"Avoiding someone?" Liam's eyebrows rose.

Yes. "It's nothing. That was the director of my company."

"Sounds important," he said tersely.

"It can wait." She cleared her throat. "Back to this recital idea. Lou really thinks that it would give us a leg up as far as getting that grant from the state?" The word *us* had flown right off her tongue without warning. She hoped Liam hadn't noticed.

Judging from the way the set of his jaw tensed, yes, he had. "He's pretty convinced, yes."

"And what do you think?" She peered up at him, waiting for an answer.

A storm of emotions passed through his gaze. Frustration. Anger. And a sadness so deep that it made Posy want to bury her face in the softness of his pine-needle scent again. "It doesn't matter what I think."

"Yes, it does. You're the youth pastor. This is your program." A recital would be difficult enough to pull off, even with Liam's support. If he were opposed to the idea, she wouldn't have a chance.

He sighed. "It's possible that a dance recital might give us an edge."

She could tell how much it pained him to admit it. No matter how happy the girls were, no matter how hard she worked, he would never get on board with the whole ballet thing, would he? He'd probably have an aneurysm if ballet lessons ever became a permanent fixture in Aurora.

Then again, there was no danger of such a thing happening. Was there?

She swallowed. "I'll do it."

Liam sighed again. "You sure about this?"

"Absolutely." She nodded.

She had three weeks left in Alaska. Three weeks for her foot to heal. Three weeks to somehow come up with ballet shoes, costumes, music, a venue and choreography, all without spending a nickel. Three weeks to teach the girls how to dance without holding on to the backs of metal folding chairs for balance.

Lord, please give me strength.

Seven pairs of ballet shoes would also be helpful.

Chapter Twelve

"So what do you think, Dr. Cooper?" Posy stretched out on the examination table in the cramped room the following morning and stared at her foot.

If ankle sprains and fractures of the fifth metatarsal could heal simply from the force of a stare, she would have been good to go. Every pair of eyes in the tiny exam room was glued to her foot, and there were a lot of eyes.

This time her mom had insisted on making the trip to Anchorage with her and Zoey. Posy couldn't very well say no. If her mother wanted to come, that was fine. If anything, maybe it would prove to her mom that she truly didn't have anything to hide.

But it did make for a rather crowded doctor's office.

"Well, let's take a look, shall we?" Dr. Cooper smiled and rested his hands on her cast.

Zoey shot Posy a look of encouragement over the top of the doctor's head. Her mother stood beside her, looking as though she might faint. Posy felt slightly sick herself all of a sudden.

This was it. The first big step toward getting her promotion. If the cast didn't come off today, there was no way she'd be ready to dance in three weeks. Even if she did manage to rid herself of it, she still wasn't certain she'd be ready in time.

"Your range of motion has definitely improved." Dr. Cooper turned her foot one direction and then the other, back and forth.

Posy winced. Her range of motion may have improved, but the ligament was still tender. That was to be expected, though, right?

She hoped so. She really hoped so.

Dr. Cooper's expression remained neutral as he continued the examination. Her inability to discern his thought process was maddening. Posy resumed staring at her foot in order to stop herself from trying to read his mind.

Over three weeks had passed since she'd taken her fall during *Cinderella*. Twenty-three days, to be precise. And still she hadn't grown accustomed to seeing her foot frozen in a flexed position within the confines of the plaster cast.

She typically never went twenty-three minutes without pointing her toes, never mind twenty-three days. She'd surely lost some of the flexibility in her foot during its incubation period. If the cast did indeed come off, she'd need to spend long sessions every day exercising with the elastic bands that she always kept in the side pocket of her dance bag. Even then, she wasn't sure her foot would have the same suppleness or the deep arch that it had before.

She took a deep breath and reminded herself not to skip too far ahead. First things first.

"Well? How does it look?" she asked.

Dr. Cooper smiled. "It looks to me like you've done exactly as I asked."

"I have. I promise."

"Do you also promise to keep up the treatment if I remove this cast for you? The temptation at first will be to jump right back into your usual activities, but you can't.

If you do, you're going to end up right back in plaster. I don't want that. I presume you don't, either."

"No." She shook her head. "Absolutely not."

"Okay, then. I think it's safe to spring you from this cumbersome thing." He rapped on her cast with his knuckles as if he were knocking on a door.

"That's wonderful news. Just wonderful." Her mother beamed.

Zoey's smile was a mile wide.

Posy wanted to join in the celebration. She really did. But she still had a very important question. The most important one of all. "Can I dance?"

Dr. Cooper crossed his arms and regarded her carefully. "You understand the importance of periods of rest?"

"Yes. Yes, I do." She nodded.

"And you'll be extra careful? No snowball fights, ice-skating, skiing, snowshoeing or jumping off buildings."

"Jumping off buildings?" Posy's brow furrowed.

Dr. Cooper shrugged. "It was the most dangerous thing I could think of off the top of my head. You get the point, right?"

"Right." She had no desire to do any of those things. Liam and the boys were scheduled to play in their first snowball match later that afternoon, and this time she had zero intention of charging onto the field.

She just wanted to dance. That was all.

Oh, and choreograph and plan a recital for a group of novice teenage ballerinas in three weeks' time. Even if she possessed a burning desire to jump off a building, she wouldn't be able to squeeze it into her busy schedule.

"Then yes. You can dance."

Those were the words she'd waited weeks to hear. The words she'd prayed for. Posy felt almost sick with relief. *Thank You, Lord.*

"But I can't place enough stress on the importance of

starting back slowly. Very slowly. Ten minutes at a time, twice a day. If that works, you can increase the time every day by small intervals. No more than five minutes more each time. Got it?"

Ten minutes, twice a day. That was nothing. But tallying up the math in her head, she figured by the time the audition rolled around, she should be able to get through it. Barely. "Got it."

"And your prescriptions? How are you doing on those? Do you need a refill of either the anti-inflammatory or the pain meds?" He whipped the dreaded prescription pad from his pocket.

Posy glanced at her mother, who'd gone suddenly white as a sheet. No doubt her mind was filled with imagined shoe boxes full of pills shoved beneath Posy's bed.

"Actually—" Posy aimed her gaze back at Dr. Cooper "—I never filled them."

"You didn't?"

"She didn't." Zoey shook her head. "She gave the prescription to me."

Dr. Cooper's gaze swiveled back and forth between the two of them. "I don't understand."

"I didn't want to take them. That's all. I had a, um, problem with pills once. I don't want to do that again." The admission, so difficult to get out, scratched against her throat. She had sounded hoarse when she'd given voice to it, but she'd said it. That was the important thing. She'd admitted it out loud.

In front of her mother.

Dr. Cooper gave her knee a reassuring squeeze; however, it was the peace Posy saw shining in her mom's eyes that was the biggest comfort of all.

"I suppose we won't be needing this, then, will we?" Dr. Cooper shoved his prescription pad back in his pocket.

"On to more important things. Are you ready to get back into your dancing shoes?"

Posy didn't hesitate. "Absolutely."

Posy wrinkled her nose. Anya's SUV smelled like dog. Like Liam's dog, to be specific. Like a big, furry, Alaskan-sized dog.

Maybe that was because there was a tiny puppy head poking out of the top of the backpack situated next to her in the backseat. The pup was copper-colored, with a tiny white dot on the top of its head. And despite the obvious fact that it was an infant in dog years, it was infinitely better behaved than Liam's monster. Case in point—the backpack was still in one piece.

"Has the entire town gone dog-crazy since I've been gone?" she asked. The puppy cocked its head at the sound of her voice.

Zoey swiveled backward in the passenger seat and grinned at the dog. "That's no ordinary puppy. He's going to grow to be an avalanche rescue dog. Anya and her husband train them."

"Really? Wow." No wonder he was so well behaved. "Liam's dog could use your help."

Anya met her gaze in the rearview mirror. "Liam has a dog? Since when?"

"I've no idea. And it's really more of a bear than a dog." A naughty, garbage-eating bear.

"I heard it ate his mattress." Zoey nodded. "And the front seat of his Jeep."

Posy found this news more amusing than she probably should have. "Where on earth did you hear that?"

Zoey shrugged. "The coffee bar at the Northern Lights, which is pretty much where I get all my news."

"Well, if it's true, I can probably give him a few tips about how to make that dog behave." Anya laughed. "Or at the very least, get him to stop eating furniture and ve-hicles."

"Good luck with that." Posy snorted in a most unballetic fashion. Then the SUV pulled to a stop, and she realized where they'd been headed. "The skating pond? You've got to be kidding."

Anya shifted the car into Park. "We wanted to sur-prise you."

"Are you surprised?" Zoey unclicked her seat belt.

"Very." Posy looked out the window at the pond that, like so many things in Aurora, felt both familiar and new at once.

It was the same oblong pond, surrounded by the same cluster of evergreens, the same frozen skeleton trees. The tiny building that housed the sound system and the mod-est snack bar was standing, but had been painted cherry red. And someone had made the lovely addition of row upon row of tiny glimmering fairy lights strung across the pond in loopy swags. Those lights changed the look and feel of everything. She imagined skating beneath them would make the snow flurries feel as though they were falling from the stars.

Of course, she'd never know, because it wasn't as if she could actually go ice-skating. She'd been out of her cast for a matter of hours. Not to mention the fact that she hadn't slipped her feet into a pair of skates in over half a decade. She wasn't even allowed to wear her pointe shoes yet.

No unnecessary risks. Wasn't that what Dr. Cooper had advised? No snowball fights. No skiing. No snow-shoeing. No skating.

It sort of looked like fun, though.

Don't even think about it.

Missing out on these things had never bothered her be-fore, and it shouldn't now. She had a career to think about. A career that most ballet dancers would kill for.

"Um, you guys, are you sure this is such a great idea? I can't even skate. Surely there's something else we can do for girls' night." Like sit around with her foot elevated or work on her Thera-Band exercises.

Although she'd already been doing that for the better part of the day. The only stretch of time that she'd been on her feet had been at ballet class this afternoon, which had been by far the best two hours of her day.

The girls were positively ecstatic about the recital. And since they had only three weeks to put something together, she'd moved them away from barre exercises and started them on center floor work for the second half of class. She'd started simple, with a basic port de bras to get them accustomed to balancing themselves without the support of their chairs. But she couldn't very well choreograph a recital consisting solely of arm movements. So then she'd started them on jetés. One by one they'd flown across the length of the fellowship hall. By the end of the hour, their smiles had grown as big as their leaps.

She still had no clue how to turn their modest skills into recital choreography, but it had been a beginning. And they had to start somewhere.

"Surely you want to see the pond before you leave to go back to California," Zoey said.

"Besides, this is Aurora, remember? Our girls'-night options are pretty limited." Anya climbed out of the SUV and shut the door.

So this is happening.

Posy reached for her purse and caught a glimpse of her cell phone in its side pocket. A missed-call reminder flashed on the tiny screen. Gabriel had called again while she'd been teaching, and in the wake of the girls' excitement about the recital, she'd completely forgotten to call him back.

She rattled off a quick text message, following up on

the one she'd finally sent yesterday after Dr. Cooper removed her cast.

Sorry I missed your call again. My foot is getting stronger every day.

Her fingertips paused over the tiny keyboard before she added a quick

I'm counting down the days until I return!

She pressed Send and tossed the phone back in her bag.

"Anya's right, Posy. It was either the skating pond or the coffee bar at the Northern Lights, and we've already been there twice since you've been back," Zoey said.

"Yes, but isn't the third time supposed to be the charm?" Posy slid out of the backseat and tried not to think about what Dr. Cooper would say if he could see her right now.

She would not skate under any circumstances. She'd sit on the bleachers and watch. Maybe she could even elevate her foot at the same time.

"Come on. It'll be fun. Besides, we need to celebrate the freedom of your foot from that awful cast." Zoey stopped at one of the benches that lined the pond and sat to put on her skates. Anya followed suit.

Zoey was right. The removal of Posy's cast was definitely an occasion for celebration. Although she felt a tad guilty celebrating after what had happened to Liam and his snowball team at the match earlier.

They'd lost in a landslide of Alaska-sized proportions. The other team had been made up entirely of older teens. Older teens who'd obviously done that sort of thing before. It had been an epic, snowy disaster.

And now Posy stood watching her friends lacing up

their skates and felt a pang of envy. *Don't be silly. You haven't even thought about skating in years.*

"Why don't you go grab some hot chocolate from the snack bar?" Zoey said. She had an oddly wide-eyed look on her face. Faux innocence.

"What's going on?" Posy asked.

Zoey and Anya exchanged glances.

"Nothing." Anya stared a little too hard at her skates as she laced them up. "Hot chocolate sounds good, though. Will you bring me a cup?"

"Sure." Posy stood there for a minute, waiting for them to make eye contact with her once again. Neither one of them did.

Since when did putting on skates require such intense concentration? She could have sewn the ribbons on three pairs of pointe shoes in the time it took them to get their skates laced up. "All right. I'll be back in a few."

She walked in the direction of the snack bar and glanced at the ice. Skaters glided in an organized circle, laughing, their breath dancing in wispy puffs in the cold Alaskan air. Posy recognized several teens from youth group. Ava, Hannah, Emily, plus a few of the boys whose names she hadn't yet learned. The boy that seemed to alternate between hovering adoringly around Melody and tormenting her was there, wearing an earnest expression and skating around the perimeter on black skates, helping small children who had fallen and admonishing the reckless ones to slow down. He wore a black-and-white-striped hat like the one Liam had worn back in high school when he was the rink referee. Something about seeing him in action made her wistful.

Lord, is there no escaping the memories in this place?

"Posy."

She tore her gaze from the movement on the pond

and aimed it toward the person manning the snack bar. "Liam?"

Touché, Lord.

For the life of him, Liam couldn't figure out what Posy was doing at the pond. It wasn't as though she could skate. Since she'd been back, he'd come to think of his skating rink as the one place he was sure never to run into her.

"What are you doing here?" she asked, frowning. Apparently, she hadn't anticipated running into him, either. "You told me you didn't work here anymore."

He shook his head. "I never said that."

"Yes, you did. On my very first day back, right after you, um…"

"Saved you from the imaginary bear?" He lifted a brow.

Her cheeks went pink. "Saved me from your marauding dog."

The dog. Where was the dog? Liam searched the crowd and spotted him sprawled on his massive belly, pond-side, decimating another one of the red plastic buckets that Ronnie used for hauling water to repair ruts in the ice. Super.

"I never said I didn't work here. I simply asked if you thought I did. There's a difference." Liam passed two cups of hot chocolate over her shoulder to the couple waiting behind her. A line was beginning to form. "Besides, I don't technically work here."

"Oh, I see. So I'm imagining things? Like the bear?"

Cute. It was good to see she was getting her sense of humor back, even if the barbs were oftentimes directed at him. "I don't work here. I own the place."

She blinked wordlessly.

Liam passed more hot chocolate over her shoulder. "Cat got your tongue?"

"Sorry. I'm surprised, that's all. You own the skating rink now? And you're the youth pastor. That's impressive,

Liam. Really." She looked at him, and for the first time since she'd come home, he felt like someone other than the boy she'd known in high school.

"Thank you."

They stood there for a moment, neither one of them saying anything until Liam remembered that, yes, even though he owned the place, he was still manning the snack bar at the moment. "Did you, uh, want anything?"

"Oh. Oh, yes, of course. Two hot chocolates, please. Anya and Zoey sent me over here, and now I'm beginning to suspect I know why."

Zoey again.

I saw the kiss, Liam.

Not only did he have to go and kiss Posy, but he'd somehow chosen to do it in front of her best friend from high school. Although in reality, it hadn't been a choice so much as a reaction to the situation. A reflex.

A mistake. Most definitely a mistake.

Now Zoey was playing matchmaker, and she'd recruited Anya to help. Just what he needed.

Liam's gut churned. "I'll get those two hot chocolates right away. I just need to change the music first."

How long had the place gone silent? Out on the pond, the skaters were still moving in unending circles. Their laughter and the scratch of their blades as they slid over the ice were louder, exaggerated without the music from the antiquated sound system Liam had installed.

Truth be told, it was a bit of exaggeration to even think of it as a sound system. By the time he'd gotten around to thinking about music, the money he had to spend on the skating pond was running thin. Until he could afford something better, he'd been forced to make do with an ancient turntable and some secondhand speakers. Every time he put a record on, he felt as if he'd stepped into another era. Which sort of made sense at the moment. Time—

past, present, future—seemed to have a way of blurring together whenever Posy was around.

He turned and lifted the needle on the record player to stop its endless motion, removed the shiny black vinyl album and replaced it with another. Over the speakers, sound crackled to life—a moment of scratchy anticipation followed by the crooning of Frank Sinatra.

He spun back around and handed Posy her two drinks. She took the paper cups, but didn't make a move to leave. Instead, she stood there, staring.

Liam frowned. "Did you need anything else?"

"Where did you get that?" She pointed at something behind him.

He followed the direction of her gaze. "The record player?"

"Yes. The record player." There was an edge to her voice, and her hand trembled slightly. The liquid sloshed over the rim of one of the cups she held.

"At the church thrift store. It's ancient, but I guess that goes without saying."

"The thrift store? I suppose that means it once belonged to someone here in town."

Liam shrugged. "Probably."

"Ouch." She dropped one of the cups, and hot chocolate spilled all over the counter. "Oh, no. I'm sorry. Here, let me help you clean that up."

"It's okay. I can do it." He reached for a towel.

"Liam, I'm holding up the line. Let me help."

Before he could stop her, she'd pushed through the swinging door of the shed and was standing beside him. In the space of the time that he'd cleaned up the spill, she'd filled cups of hot chocolate for three people and handed out two bags of popcorn.

"Thanks," he said. "It's always crazy busy this time of night."

"You're welcome." She smiled and kept lining up cups, pouring drinks, making change.

Liam didn't have the luxury of time to feel awkward about her helping out behind the counter. He was grateful for the assistance. Besides, they'd been working together at the church for the past few weeks without managing to strangle each other, albeit not quite in such close proximity.

For the next half hour or so, they worked side by side until the line slowed. Customers showed up fewer and further between until finally it was time to close up shop.

Posy blinked as he slid the closed sign in place. "Closed? Already?"

"Take a look." Liam nodded toward the pond, vacant now, save for Melody executing a perfect spin in the center of the ice and a lone figure standing on the edge watching. Ronnie.

"Look at that! That's a beautiful arabesque." Posy narrowed her gaze. "Who's the skater?"

"Melody."

"Melody? As in, Melody from ballet class?"

Liam clenched his jaw. "Melody. As in, Melody from youth group."

The last time he'd checked, it was still a church, not a ballet school.

She jammed her hands on her hips. "Why didn't you tell me she could do that?"

"Skate?"

"No. Dance." Something about the way she said it caused alarm bells to go off in Liam's head.

"She's not a dancer. She's a skater. She has a coach up in Anchorage on the weekends, but skates here during the week."

"She mentioned something to me the other day about skating practice, and today her jetés were awfully impressive for a beginner, but I had no idea she could do...that."

Posy gestured toward the ice, where Melody was gliding in a smooth circle, balanced on one leg with the other
stretched out behind her.

"Liam, this is perfect." Posy clapped her hands. She
seemed wholly unconcerned about the fact that her friends
were nowhere to be seen and that Liam would have to give
her a ride home, a detail which he was certain had been
carefully orchestrated by Anya and Zoey.

"What do you mean?" he asked.

"She's the answer." Posy grinned.

She was up to something. He could sense it. Whatever
that something was, it was sure to make him even more
uncomfortable than the thought of giving her an innocent ride home.

He crossed his arms. "I must have missed the question.
What are you talking about?"

"I'm talking about the dance recital, silly."

Of course. All ballet. All the time. "Oh. That."

"Maybe I can feature her in a dance." She was getting
that faraway look—the one that meant her thoughts were
whirling on pink-satin tiptoe and he may as well not exist.
Which was fine.

If it's so fine, why does it bother you so much?

In the center of the ice, Melody slowed to a stop. She
waved a mittened hand at Ronnie, still watching from the
edge of the pond. He waved back. But when she skated
toward him, he turned tail and stomped away.

"Did you see that?" Posy frowned. "I can't figure out if
those two like each other or despise one another. What's
with them?"

Young love.

"Your guess is as good as mine." Liam shook his head.
Beside him, Posy grew pensive. Quiet.

"Thank you again for all the help tonight." She'd been
on her feet for a long time. Too long. It couldn't have been

good for her foot, but as usual, neither one of them broached the subject out loud. "I'll give you a lift home, since it looks like you've been abandoned."

Her cheeks colored. The fact that Anya and Zoey had left her there was no accident. Posy knew it as surely as he did.

"I just need to go talk to Ronnie for a minute before we head out. Why don't you sit down and rest?"

"Okay. And Liam…" She gave him a thoughtful glance. One that told him that possibly, just possibly, she was thinking about something other than dance. "Thank you."

"I should be thanking *you*. You just pulled a two-hour shift behind this counter."

"It was fun, actually." Beneath the golden glow of the lights strung overhead, he could see her cheeks turn instantly rosy. She cleared her throat. "I mean, what else was I going to do? It's not like I could skate or anything."

Was he imagining things, or was there a hint of longing in her voice? "Yeah, I guess not."

She glanced at the mirror surface of the ice, empty now that Melody had gone. A smile tipped her lips, and for a moment, Liam could almost see skaters from years ago gliding and spinning in the reflection of her gaze.

He was losing it. Clearly. "I'm going to go talk to Ronnie now. I'll be right back."

A little space. A little distance. That was what he needed. *Like the distance from here to San Francisco?*

That was a thought he didn't want to contemplate. Not yet. But it wasn't as though he had a choice. She was leaving whether he was ready or not.

He was ready. Of course he was ready.

Chapter Thirteen

Posy sank onto one of the benches at the edge of the pond to wait for Liam. She rotated her ankle a few times and was pleasantly surprised to find it no more tender than it had been earlier in the day. She probably shouldn't have been on her feet for so long tonight, but the time had passed quicker than she'd realized.

It had been nice helping Liam. Nicer than working with him at the church, where they pretty much avoided each other as much as possible. She wondered what that meant, if anything.

Stop overanalyzing things. It's good to be friends.

Friends. Was that what they were, what they'd become? Most likely, which was a good thing. Friends were important. Everyone needed friends.

Then why did the idea make her feel so profoundly sad?

She tried not to dwell on the matter and instead concentrated on pointing her toes, inasmuch as she could point them in her snow boots. She swished her foot through the snow in the shape of a half circle, executing a perfect, seated rond de jambe. The familiar motion took the edge off her worry, as barre exercises always did.

But as calming as she found the movement, Liam's dog

thought otherwise. He bounded toward her, nose to the ground, tail wagging, and pawed at her foot.

"Hey there," she said. And then, as more of an experiment than anything else, she added, "Sit."

The dog cocked its head and plunked its rear on the snowy ground in a perfect sit position.

Posy smiled. "Well, what do you know? I suppose you're not all bad, are you?"

He let out a happy-sounding bark and panted, his massive pink tongue lolling out of the side of his mouth. He wasn't such a monster, really. She'd noticed him creeping into her ballet classes every now and then. Yes, he had a tendency to overturn chairs whenever he was around, but she supposed that could simply be a result of his size. Really, did Liam have to choose such an enormous dog? Weren't there any Chihuahuas in Alaska, or was that strictly a California breed?

The dog stood. Posy told him to sit, and once again, he obeyed.

"Good boy," she said and gave him a pat on the head as a reward. "You know what? I don't even know your name."

She glanced at the red collar around his neck and checked it for a tag. Sure enough, she found one buried among the dog's thick, wooly coat. She tried to read the name etched on it, but had trouble seeing in the dim light. It appeared to start with an *S*. Or was that a *P*?

She turned the tag this way and that, until it caught a ray of light and she was able to make out the first letter. An *S*. Then the next two. A *U*, followed by an *N*.

S-U-N.

At the sight of those letters, Posy's throat grew dry. She knew the rest without even looking at them. But she squinted at the tag in the darkness anyway. She wanted to see the word. She *needed* to see it.

She bent closer and brushed the dog's dark fur out of

the way. And there it was. She didn't know why Liam had chosen the name or what it meant. But it meant something. She was sure it did.

There was still so much she didn't understand. But at that moment, the only thing that mattered was the glow of warmth that this newfound secret kindled in her soul. A warmth that felt oddly like coming home. "It's nice to officially meet you, Sundog."

Liam caught up with Ronnie just as he cranked the engine of his dilapidated truck to life.

Thinking of it as dilapidated was actually being rather generous. The outside was so weather-beaten that Liam couldn't tell what color the original paint job had been. What parts weren't rusted through simply appeared to be a generic metal color. And the interior looked as if it had played host to an entire family of Sundogs. It was a miracle the thing ran.

Liam knocked on the driver's-side window.

Ronnie rolled it down. "Oh, hi, Pastor. I thought it was okay to leave since everyone had gone home. Do you need something?"

"No." Liam shook his head. "I just thought we should talk."

"Um, now?"

"Now. Yes." Liam shrugged. "It should only take a minute. And don't worry. You're not in trouble. I only wanted to ask you about what happened back there with Melody."

"Nothing. I watched her skate. You told me I should, so I did." Ronnie's shoulders sagged.

"And?"

"And she was good, just like you said. Really good." The tone of his voice was wholly at odds with the words coming out of his mouth.

"Ronnie, be straight with me. I know you like Melody,

and I'm pretty sure she likes you, too. So what's the problem here?"

"The problem is how good she is." Ronnie looked Liam square in the eyes, and in that instant, it all became crystal clear.

Liam got it. Finally. He understood Ronnie. Not all that long ago, Liam had *been* Ronnie. "You're worried she's going to leave, aren't you?"

Ronnie shrugged. "Maybe."

Never had a *maybe* sounded so much like a resounding *yes*. "I understand."

Ronnie's brow furrowed. "You do?"

More than you know.

"Yeah, I do." He took a deep breath and tried not to sound like the biggest impostor in the world, which was an awfully tall order. "But you can't worry about that now."

"How can I not worry? We're graduating next year. She wants to train for the Olympics. There's some training place in Germany I heard her talking about. Germany. Do you know how far away that is?"

Four thousand miles, give or take. Although perhaps now wasn't the best time to point out the measured distance. "You're getting ahead of yourself, kid. You're worrying about things that may never happen."

"But what if they do?" Ronnie peered up at him, and in the depths of his wide-eyed youth, Liam saw a spark of hope amid the sadness. Hope that Liam could fix things, that he would have all the answers.

Lord, help me out here.

"The future is messy, Ronnie. I wish I could tell you it wasn't. I wish I could tell you that you could spend time planning your future and that if you did everything right, all your plans would fall neatly into place. And I wish I could tell you that what you wanted would always fall in

line with what the people you care about want, as well."
Oh, how he wished that.

He wanted the best for Ronnie. He wanted the best for
all the kids. But was an easy, predictable future really
best for anyone?

Ronnie sighed.

"No one knows what the future holds. Not me, not you
and not Melody," Liam went on. "That's one of the great-
est joys of being human. What fun would life be without
its surprises, its unexpected twists and turns?"

Surprises, unexpected twists and turns. Like Posy leaving...like Posy coming back.

He swallowed. "Don't let fear of the future stop you
from caring about someone. You could miss out on something, on some*one*, who will change your life forever. Do
you understand what I'm saying?"

"Yes, Pastor. I do." Ronnie nodded. "It's just hard."

"I know it is. Think about it, though, okay? And in the
meantime, try to be nice to Melody."

"I will." He shifted the truck into gear.

Liam stepped back a few feet and waved. "Have a good
night. You did a great job today at the snowball fight, by
the way."

Ronnie shook his head. "But we lost."

"It was never about winning." It had been about team-
work. About fun.

And maybe a little bit about winning, but only inasmuch as winning would have given him a better shot at
being awarded the grant money he so desperately wanted
for the youth group. At least they still had a shot at it with
Posy's recital.

Please, God. Let that recital be a success.

He cleared his throat. What was he doing? He was worrying about the future, right after he'd encouraged Ronnie

to live in the moment. Why did he ever think he could be a proper role model for these kids?

"Good night, Ronnie," he said.

Ronnie gave him a halfhearted wave, rolled up the window and drove away.

Liam stood, watching him drive away, and wondered if what he'd said to the boy made him a hypocrite. Sure, it had sounded great. And the truth was, he believed every word of it. He believed in the joys and surprises of life. Those things were a gift from God. Blessings to be held tightly and cherished.

Then what am I doing?

He shoved his hands in his pockets and searched for Posy through the dizzying flurry of snowflakes. He found her in the distance sitting on one of the benches at the edge of the pond, moving her delicately arched foot in graceful circles on the snowy ground. The familiarity of the movement grabbed him by the throat. How many times had he seen her draw patterns on the floor with those toes of hers? Countless. Sitting in the bleachers at his baseball games, at her desk at school, even nestled beside him in the junker of a car—vaguely reminiscent of Ronnie's—that he'd driven in twelfth grade. He doubted she was consciously aware of it. It seemed purely instinctual, the way her feet were in constant motion. As if she'd been dancing someplace far away, even as she'd sat right beside him

He'd been so young then. Almost the same age as Ronnie. Too young to deal with the hand he'd been dealt—a girl he loved bent on destroying herself, coupled with the choice to follow his parents off on another adventure or stay and make a home in Aurora. Alone. All while he was still only in his teens.

How different would things have turned out if he and Posy had been older? If the events of the past had instead taken place now. Today.

Sometimes it felt uncannily as though they were.

He walked toward Posy through the flurry of the late-night snowfall, surprised when he grew closer and saw Sundog sitting calmly at her feet. The dog stood and wagged his tail when he saw Liam approaching. Then Posy said something to him, and he sat again.

"What's this?" Liam asked as he grew closer. "A secret double? Because this can't be my dog. I've never seen him sit still for this long without simultaneously destroying something."

"I assure you he's yours." She glanced up at him. There was an openness in her gaze that hadn't been there moments ago when they'd been manning the snack bar together. "This is Sundog."

Memories swirled amid the snowflakes. A tree. A whisper. A kiss.

He held out his hand. "Come skate with me."

"Skate with you?" She shook her head. "You know I can't."

"Trust me, Posy." *Trust me. One last time.*

The trees surrounding the pond all held their breath and the snow flurries hung in the air, suspended, as Liam stood there offering her his hand. Ever so slowly, she smiled and placed her hand in his.

"Come on." He pulled her to her feet.

Hand in hand, they walked to the snack bar, where he put another record on the record player and slipped his feet into his skates.

Posy watched him wordlessly, and for once the silence between them didn't feel loaded with bittersweet sadness. He laced up his skates, every one of his senses kicking into overdrive. He was hyperaware of Posy's gaze on him, the whisper of the cold winter breeze on his hands and face, and the breathless feeling of anticipation that lingered between the moment he set the needle on the record and the one in which the music came to life. An oldies ballad. The kind of song that couples swayed to long ago, back when slow dancing was still in style.

Once he was laced up, he stood and took her hand again. "Ready?"

She gave him a curious smile. "Maybe."

"I told you to trust me. Come on."

He led her to the pond, walking slowly through the rapidly accumulating snow so she wouldn't slip and hurt herself again. When they reached the ice, he stepped onto its smooth crystal surface. Maybe this was a crazy idea, and maybe he would regret it a month from now after she'd gone. But for right now, he wanted to heed his own advice and savor the moment. Live his life. Follow his heart. And what his heart most wanted was to dance with Posy Sutton.

"Dance with me." He gave her hand a gentle tug and pulled her toward him.

He didn't need to tell her what to do. She already knew. How, he wasn't sure. They'd never danced like this before. In fact, they'd never danced together, period. Dance had always been her thing and hers alone. Something that separated the two of them more often than it brought them closer together. At school dances, he'd been too intimidated to dance with her. Music had never moved him the way it did through Posy.

But now was different. He was different, and so was she.

Gingerly, she placed her feet on top of his so that she was facing him, standing on the boots of his skates, like a child first learning how to dance. She rested one hand on his shoulder and kept the other entwined with his. She looked up at him, and Liam watched as her graceful composure and staged confidence fell away. He was no longer a man looking at a dancer. He was a man looking at a woman.

"It's about time you asked me to dance," she murmured.

Her upturned face was so close to his that their frosty breath commingled in the glacial Alaskan air. He looked into those gray eyes that were so often filled with storms and saw nothing but an elegant tranquillity, like the lifting of an evening fog.

She was beautiful. So beautiful. She always had been, but Liam didn't want to dance with a memory, a reflection of the past, no matter how lovely and familiar. He wanted something real. He wanted to dance with the grown woman Posy had become. The woman in his arms.

"I was waiting for the right moment," he said, gliding his foot along the ice.

She laughed and tightened her grip on him as he moved them over the frozen mirror of the pond, linked foot to foot and hand to hand. Slowly at first, and rather shyly. But as the music played on, Liam's movements grew bolder, quicker. Soon they were spinning and floating with the wind whipping through their hair until it was no longer Liam guiding their steps, but the music.

He felt it.

At last.

The music, the freedom. The feeling of movement being something of beauty, a work of art. He understood.

Somehow, someway, after all this time, Posy had taught him what it meant to dance.

He knew it didn't change anything. In a matter of weeks, they would go their separate ways. The past might belong to them, but the future never would. Nothing had changed.

Yet somehow, everything had. Because they'd created the perfect moment. A new memory that would live forever. This dance hadn't been about trying to hold on to something. It had been about letting something go. Letting *her* go.

He'd been ready to offer Posy all the love in the world back then, but what would that have mattered if she'd been unhappy? How long would it have taken for the screaming fury of young love to wither to a whisper if she'd chosen him over dance? If she'd stayed.

He wanted more for her. More than Alaska. More than a love that put shackles on her dancing feet. He wanted her to have everything.

"Liam," she whispered. "After all of this is over, maybe…"

Don't. Don't say it.

"Let's not talk about tomorrows. Not now." He didn't want her yesterdays, and he didn't have a place in her tomorrows. But now, beneath the star-swept Alaskan sky, the snow fell just for them. This moment was theirs and theirs alone. "Dance with me. Here. Now."

Meet me. Meet me here, Posy.

He pulled her closer, gazed into her eyes and waited with his heart in his throat as she stepped into the moment. Memories and expectations lifted away, like a shimmering veil. And it was in the subtle, gentle parting of her lips that she left the past behind and the future to its own devices.

"You're beautiful," he whispered as his skates came to a stop with an agonizingly slow scrape against the ice.

Then the two of them stopped moving, and it was the world that kept on spinning in a dizzying snow-shaker swirl. Liam tried to take it all in—the glittering gold stars, the diamond snowflakes that had gathered in Posy's coppery hair, the way she was looking at him as if he were the only man that ever did, ever could or ever would matter.

And in that moment of innocent grace, Liam lowered his lips to hers.

It was like kissing his past, present and future all at once. Everything he'd ever wanted was wrapped up and tied with ribbons in that tender meeting of their lips. Their mouths were frosty cold, and snow flurries whipped around them as they stood on the mirrored surface of the ice, but there was warmth in Liam's heart. Warmth, tenderness and an ache so fierce that his chest felt as if it were being ripped in two.

There were so many things he wanted to say. Words danced on the tip of his tongue. Dangerous words that he had no business saying aloud. Words like *mine* and *love*. And the most dangerous word of all—*stay*. It was a mighty struggle to hold them back.

Think of her happiness. Think of her.

He kissed her again. And again. And this time he was kissing each one of her dreams, willing them to come true.

Then on and on they skated, until the record stopped and the needle came to its noiseless end. In the center of the pond, Liam's feet spun them into a whisper-silent twirl. Round and round they went until the momentum died and they slowed to a halt.

Posy's eyes were wild, the tip of her nose as red as a cherry. Liam had never seen her look this way before— this happy, this carefree—without a pair of ballet shoes on her feet.

"Thank you," she said, and suddenly Liam realized she was looking at him through eyes filled with glistening, unshed tears.

He released her hand and brushed the hair from her eyes before cupping her cheek. "For what, exactly?"

She blinked up at him, and a lone tear slid down her face. Her eyes had grown stormy once again. Misty gray, like a gathering tempest. Eyes filled with goodbyes.

A bittersweet heaviness settled in Liam's chest. He told himself the burning in his lungs was from the biting-cold air and the exertion of their dance. But deep down he knew it was a lie.

He wiped away her teardrop with a brush of his thumb, but the trail it left in its wake remained. As did the ache in his heart.

Her answer came in a whisper softer than the fall of snowflakes drifting onto the ice. "For the best dance lesson I've ever had."

Chapter Fourteen

"What exactly are we looking for again?" Zoey walked alongside Posy toward the entrance to the Aurora Community Church Thrift Store, juggling a cardboard tray loaded down with four cups of coffee from the Northern Lights Inn.

"Record albums," Posy said. "Remember those?"

"Vaguely." Anya frowned.

"No." Zoey shook her head. "I actually don't."

"You're kidding. I find that profoundly sad." Posy stared down at the ground as she walked, picking her way through the snow, careful to avoid any patches of ice. As happy as she was to be rid of the plaster cast, her foot felt oddly vulnerable and exposed without it. She couldn't quite get past the fear of falling.

Realistically, she knew she wasn't going to fall. The only danger of falling had been the night when Liam had taken her skating. And that had been a falling of a different variety.

Don't go there. You are not *falling in love with him. You can't.*

But no matter how hard she fought against it, she feared there was a tiny part of her heart that had already begun that rarest of descents. She could almost feel herself free-falling into an everlasting tombé.

Zoey laughed, pulling her thoughts back to the matter at hand. What was that again? Oh, right. Madame Sylvie's records.

"I'm just teasing," Zoey said. "I know what a record album is. What I don't understand is why we're on a wild-goose chase to find some."

"Try not to think of it as a wild-goose chase. It's more like a treasure hunt." Posy grinned.

She'd been telling herself all morning not to get her hopes up. Even if the record player that she'd seen the other night at the skating pond had been the one that belonged to Madame Sylvie, it didn't mean the albums would still be around. Most of them had been nothing but ballet practice music, repetitive eight counts of piano chords composed for the routine of barre exercises. Pliés, tendus, battements, rond de jambes. They weren't exactly typical fare for iPod playlists. But to Posy, they were precious. Those soothing notes sounded like her childhood, like dance itself. Like her dreams.

"Well, if anyone can help you find them, my mom can." Anya pushed through the door of the thrift shop and held it open for Zoey. She plucked one of the coffees off the tray as Zoey passed. "Give me one of those. I'm dying for some caffeine. And the smell is out of this world."

"I aim to please." Zoey handed Posy a cup. "Here, have one."

"Thanks." She took a sip. The explosion of flavor that hit her tongue was so unexpected that she stopped dead in her tracks. "What is this? I thought I was drinking coffee."

Zoey and Anya exchanged bemused glances.

"You are," Anya said.

"This is not coffee." Posy had consumed copious amounts of coffee. Ballerinas lived on coffee. Bad coffee, mediocre coffee and what she'd always thought of as good coffee. But nothing like what she held in her hand.

"Yes, it is. Specifically, it's a caramel latte." Zoey smiled, then added, "With whip."

"Let me translate that for you—normal-people coffee." Anya sipped hers again. "Good, isn't it?"

A caramel latte with whipped cream. There had to be more calories in that cup than what Posy normally consumed in an actual, edible meal. She couldn't bring herself to question the fat content of the milk. Whole milk hadn't passed her lips since she'd slipped on her first pair of pointe shoes.

Zoey set the cardboard tray beside the cash register on the counter at the entrance to the thrift shop. "Come on, Posy. Live a little. There's more to life than all ballet, all the time."

She stared into her cardboard cup. "I know that."

She'd gone ice-skating a few nights ago, hadn't she?

She took a defiant swig of her latte.

"Can I help you?" Kirimi, Anya's mother, came bustling through the narrow aisles of the shop, eyes cast down at a bundle of neatly folded clothes in her arms. When she looked up, her olive face split into a wide grin. "Girls! It's so great to see you all here. What brings you by?"

Anya gave her mom a tight hug, then handed her a latte. "Posy is looking for some music. Plus we brought you coffee."

"Thank you." She took a sip. How she didn't faint from elation was a mystery to Posy. *Normal-people coffee.* What else had she been missing out on all this time? "What kind of music do you need, Posy?"

"I'm looking for some record albums. Specific ones. They would have come here from the ballet studio that closed a few years ago."

"Oh." Kirimi's face fell. "That was a while ago. We have

some record albums, but I doubt any of them have been around that long. You're welcome to go through them. I'm afraid they're not in any kind of order. We're perpetually shorthanded around here."

Posy looked around at the crowded shelves of books, knickknacks and clothes, clothes and more clothes. She wasn't surprised to hear that the shop was shorthanded. It was obviously a lot to keep up with. But Posy couldn't help feeling as though she were standing in the middle of a treasure chest. These weren't just items from the past. Everything here represented a story. A life.

"I don't mind doing some digging," she said.

Suddenly, the opening bars of the *Swan Lake* score rang from inside her handbag. Her cell phone. It had begun to elicit a Pavlovian response in her every time it rang. One that felt vaguely like panic.

She glanced at her phone. *Incoming call: Gabriel.*

She flipped the ringer to the off position and dropped the phone back in her purse. She'd call him back later. She couldn't very well talk to him now. It would be rude.

"I'm so sorry, Kirimi." Posy smiled and pushed away thoughts of Gabriel's repeated calls. It was surprising that he seemed so interested in the progress of her recovery. Flattering, but strange.

"It's no trouble. Did you need to take that call?" Kirimi asked.

"No. It can wait." She'd call Gabriel later when she had more time. Not that she had much time to spare at the moment. Plans for the recital were eating up every free moment. "Lead the way to the records."

"Alrighty. Follow me." Kirimi led them to the back of the store, where a row of milk crates, each one crammed with record albums, were lined up on waist-high shelves. "Here you go. Good luck."

"Thanks." Posy took a fortifying sip of her coffee and took a deep breath. "Here we go."

Anya flipped through one of the crates. "I'm keeping my eyes peeled for anything with ballerinas on the cover."

"Me, too," said Zoey. "Or just anything with one of the presidents on it."

"One of the presidents?" Posy frowned.

Zoey shrugged. "You're looking for classical stuff, right? Classical composers look an awful lot like our country's Founding Fathers. Don't tell me you've never noticed the resemblance between Mozart and George Washington."

Anya paused. "Hey, you're right. Although for Washington, I'd choose Haydn. Mozart gives off more of a Jefferson vibe."

Posy shook her head and laughed. "I am most definitely no longer in the land of ballerinas."

Zoey lifted a brow. "Is that so bad?"

No, actually. It wasn't. Posy would miss this once she was gone—the camaraderie, the laughter. She would miss a lot of things.

"Speaking of ballerinas...look!" Anya grabbed a record album from her crate and triumphantly held it over her head.

Posy gasped. She recognized the record at once. Its cover was slightly more faded than it had been the last time she'd seen it, but the photograph of girls in black leotards lined up along a ballet barre, their slippered feet pointed at identical angles, was forever seared in her memory. *The Etudes II.*

She had to stop herself from automatically moving into a glissade. "Yes! That's one of them."

Anya handed her the record. "If one of them is here, then surely there are more."

They sped up the search process, and in the next fifteen

minutes, they'd gone through every crate and collected a stack of eleven albums, all of which Posy recognized. Not just with her eyes, but with her feet, her heart and her pointed toes.

"I can't believe it." She gathered the pile in her arms. The worn edges of the old records were softer than felt. "Madame Sylvie's records. All of them."

She was holding on to history.

She thought of all the endless movements her body had made to the music in her arms and of the way she still sometimes heard Madame Sylvie's rhythmic counting in her sleep. *One, two, three, four, and up, two, three, four, and plié, two, three, four...*

Then she thought of the black satin ribbon in her pointe shoe when she'd danced *Swan Lake*, and a lump lodged in her throat.

"They're your records now," Anya said.

My records. The thought made her both happy and sad at the same time. She set them on the counter and fished through her purse for her wallet.

Zoey glanced at the shelf full of CD players and old jam boxes. "Too bad there's not a record player here for sale."

In her mind, Posy saw Liam turning his back, the golden glow of the fairy lights dancing on his hair, the fall of his soft flannel shirt as it stretched across the width of his shoulders. She saw him reaching for the arm of the record player, his hands as they lifted the vinyl from the spindle and replaced it with another.

She could ask him to sell it to her. She could buy him another, nicer record player for the skating pond. But she wouldn't. It seemed appropriate that there were people moving to its melody, dancing on the ice. What would she do with it, anyway? Her foot was nearly healed. She had a life to return to. A life a world away, where Madame Sylvie's record player would sit silent, gathering dust.

The lump in her throat grew tenfold. "Yeah, too bad."

A week into rehearsals for the recital, Posy realized that the shortage of ballet apparel in Aurora was the least of her problems. In fact, all fashion-related obstacles had been eliminated on day one with a brief phone call to Martha, the costume mistress for Posy's dance company in San Francisco.

She'd pleaded the girls' case, and once Martha heard that there was a group of teenagers in Alaska who'd never had the opportunity to slip their feet into a pair of ballet slippers, she'd gone about rectifying the situation immediately. Within days, a box had arrived, packed to the brim with pale pink leather ballet shoes. They were discards from company dancers throughout the years that Martha had been holding on to for some inexplicable reason. They'd been previously worn, of course, which the girls seemed to think made them infinitely more valuable than if they'd been brand-new. In the words of Melody, they were *real* ballet shoes that had been worn by *real* dancers. Thus, they'd been deemed priceless, irrespective of the threadbare areas around the toes.

Even more surprising than the girls' steadfast affection for their hand-me-down ballet shoes were the seven sets of white leotards and matching tutus that had been buried at the bottom of the box. In those first few days of planning, costumes had been a luxury that Posy hadn't allowed herself to think about. She'd certainly never expected Martha to whip up tutus for the girls or purchase leotards and tights with company funds. But that was exactly what she'd done, with approval from the company's charitable foundation. Less than a week after Liam had approached her with the idea of putting on a recital, she'd managed to procure ballet shoes and full costumes for all seven girls. The disinterested teenagers that she'd first met just weeks ago would dance the part of winter-wonderland snowflakes.

Other details quickly fell into place, as well. The Aurora Community Center had a stage available free of charge. Posy's mother had been thrilled to put together a program on her laptop. Even her dad had decided to pitch in, agreeing to put his photography skills to use taking photos at the recital instead of chasing moose into public buildings. Posy had decided that perhaps it wasn't such a bad thing after all that the moose report on the nightly news had bitten the dust.

The problem wasn't the shoes, the costumes, the music, the staging or the programs. It wasn't even the choreography. Inspired by the snowy-white tutus, Posy had decided to put together a simple dance to the music from the Winter Fairy's Variation in *Cinderella*. She knew the music like the back of her hand since it had been her most recent performance piece. She'd just never gotten a chance to dance to it onstage since she'd fallen during the opening bars.

Even her broken foot was no longer her biggest problem. She'd been dancing in tiny increments as recommended by Dr. Cooper, and every day she felt stronger and more sure of herself.

The problem was none of these things. The problem, unfortunately, was the dancing.

It wasn't for lack of trying. Posy had done her absolute best. So had the girls. But the amount of skills that a dancer could acquire in four short weeks simply wasn't sufficient to put together a classical-ballet number. At least not one that wasn't a complete and total snooze fest.

"What do you think?" she asked Liam during rehearsal one day in the fellowship hall. "I added an eight count of tendus to that section."

Seated beside her, he was notably silent.

"Liam, I asked you a question." She swiveled in her seat to look at him, and only then did she realize that he was asleep. To add insult to injury, he started snoring when she tried to wake him.

"Liam!" She jabbed him with her elbow.

He woke with a start and jammed a hand through his hair. "What? I'm watching."

Posy rolled her eyes. "No, you aren't. You were asleep."

"I wasn't." He yawned and blinked a few times.

A mysterious noise rose above the notes of the music, and after a quick scan of the room Posy realized it was the sound of a Newfoundland snoring. Wonderful. Even Sundog was wholly unimpressed.

"This is bad. This is really bad. You're so bored you can't even stay awake." Posy glanced back at the front of the room, where the girls continued to dance.

The poor things. Their faces were scrunched in concentration, stage grins glued in place. Posy had never seen a corps of dancers so determined to perform to the best of their ability. They deserved thunderous applause and a standing ovation, both of which were unlikely to happen.

To her abject horror, she found herself yawning.

"Liam, we have to do something. This isn't going to work," she murmured. In the center of the floor, Melody was executing a shaky passé.

She'd given Melody a featured role in the dance, which had definitely helped matters. But the entire variation was just missing something. There had to be a way to breathe life into this routine. Something simple and doable, even at a beginning level. For the life of her, she couldn't come up with anything.

Liam cut her a meaningful look. "Posy, you know you're being too hard on yourself."

Maybe he was right. Maybe her unending quest for perfection—the flawless turnout, the just-right arabesque—

was getting in the way of enjoying this whole process. Ballerinas were notorious overachievers, and she was no exception. When you spent hours upon hours, days upon days, years upon years standing in front of a mirror repeating the same movements, it was all too easy to notice the slightest little wobble or imperfection.

But that didn't explain the snoring of the masses, did it?

"I want them to be happy, to be proud of themselves. They've worked so hard. I want the people in the audience to jump to their feet when it's over."

Liam smiled warmly. "They will. The show is for their friends and relatives. You know what a tight-knit community this is. You couldn't ask for a more supportive audience."

"I also want the grant for the youth program. You do, too." And therein lay the true problem. Would the recital be impressive enough to convince the government to award money to their program? Money they so desperately needed?

"I see your point." Liam's smile faded.

Despite his best efforts, the snowball team's record thus far was a dismal 0-3. The boys were having fun despite their losing streak, but Lou was even more convinced that the youth group's only shot at the grant was Posy's ballet instruction. And of course, he was sure the biggest jewel in their crown would be the recital.

Her stomach hurt just thinking about it.

"I want to capture the wonder of dance, Liam. That spirit has nothing to do with technical perfection. It's something else. Something better."

"I know," he said quietly. He was thinking about their night on the ice.

She was thinking about it, too. Because that sweet moment of magic was precisely the feeling she wanted to somehow capture within the recital. But who was she kidding? That had been a once-in-a-lifetime occurrence. Dancing with Liam had meant more to her than all of her ballet performances put together.

But she couldn't dwell on that now. Thinking that way would make leaving all the more difficult.

The music swelled. Posy squeezed her eyes closed against the images dancing and spinning in her imagination. She did her best not to sigh, not to picture herself moving across a diamond sheet of ice in Liam's arms, stepping in time to the dramatic crescendo of Prokofiev's score.

Why did she keep reliving that moment?

Because it was the single most romantic moment of your existence.

She opened her eyes.

"That's it," she said.

"What?" Liam asked.

"I've figured it out. What this recital needs is romance. Not more advanced dance steps or anything technical. Just the tenderness of romance." How had she not thought of this before? It was so simple.

"Surely you're not saying what I think you're saying."

Indeed she was.

"I'm talking about a pas de deux. It's the perfect idea. Think about it. It would look so great on the grant application. We just need one thing to make it work." She smiled. The steps were already coming to her. Basic turns, a promenade—the sweet simplicity of Cinderella dancing with her Prince Charming. "A dance partner for Melody."

Chapter Fifteen

"No way." Ronnie shook his head so hard that Liam was almost worried it would fall right off his neck. "No. Way."

"Ronnie," Liam said with exaggerated calmness. "I urge you to think about this for a little while before you say no."

He'd been worried that Ronnie's reaction wouldn't be favorable, which was why he'd convinced Posy to let him handle the situation. Liam suspected that if Posy approached him with the idea, he wouldn't be able to see past her clothes—the leotard and tights—and wonder if she would expect him to wear something similar.

Plus Liam had developed a special rapport with Ronnie. He had a feeling Ronnie would get on board simply because he asked for his help.

As added insurance, Liam had removed Ronnie from the situation. Far away from anything ballet-related. Plus he'd invoked pizza as a bribe, choosing to drop the bomb on him at the pizza parlor down the street from the church.

"No way," Ronnie said again and shoved a slice of pepperoni pizza in his mouth. "Find someone else, Pastor. Please."

So much for their special rapport.

"Ronnie, like I said before, if you just think about it…"

Ronnie gestured wildly with his pizza slice. A few shavings of pepperoni went airborne. "I don't need to think about it. There's no way I'm going to put on a pair of tights and get up onstage in front of the entire town. I can't believe you're even asking me to do this. Haven't I been punished enough? It was one snowball. *One snowball!*"

To say he wasn't taking the news well that Posy wanted him to dance the role of Prince Charming in the recital would have been an understatement. An understatement bigger than the imaginary bear Posy had thought was after her on her first day back in town.

"Think about the group for a minute, Ronnie. Think about how hard the girls have been working on this recital." He paused for dramatic effect before he pulled out the big guns. If this didn't work, nothing would. "Think about Melody."

Ronnie's second pizza slice paused halfway en route to his mouth. "What about Melody?"

Finally they were getting somewhere. "She would be your dance partner."

"She would?" he asked tentatively.

"Yes. She's Cinderella, and you'd be playing the part of Prince Charming."

Ronnie frowned. "Are you sure? I thought Posy was the big star of the show. She's the famous dancer and all. Isn't she supposed to be Cinderella?"

"I'm one hundred percent sure. Posy is only dancing in the recital because Pastor Lou insisted that she participate. She's going to dance a small solo at the very end. The show is really about you kids." Liam slid a slice of pizza onto his plate before it was too late. Ronnie was putting away the food faster than the snow was falling outside. "Melody is most definitely Cinderella."

"And I would get to dance with her? Like it was prom?"

Ah, prom. Liam had forgotten all about it. The big high school dance was still two months away, but that hadn't stopped the kids from chatting about it nearly every day at youth group.

"Not exactly like prom, but similar. It's still ballet, but maybe Melody would be more inclined to go to prom with you if she danced with you in the recital. That's certainly something to consider." He needed to consider it fast. The recital was only a week and a half away.

"I don't know, Pastor. Me? Ballet? I just don't see it."

"All right. I understand." Liam feigned nonchalance. He was down to his final tactic. "I'm sure one of the other boys will step up to the plate."

Ronnie kept on eating, but then seemed to catch on to the implications of what Liam had said. "Wait. What do you mean one of the other boys? I thought Posy wanted me to do it."

"She does, but if you say no, she's going to ask someone else. Caleb probably. He and Melody get along great. They'd make a good couple, don't you think?" He was laying it on a little thick, but desperate times called for desperate measures.

"Fine." Ronnie tossed a sliver of pizza crust down on his plate. "I'll do it."

"I thought you might change your mind." Liam grinned. *"But no tights!"*

The next afternoon, Liam busied himself in his office while Posy held the first rehearsal for the pas de deux she'd choreographed for Melody and Ronnie. He'd offered to help out to make sure Ronnie cooperated as promised, but Posy had assured him that his assistance wasn't necessary. She could handle things on her own, which was for the best, really. He had plenty to do. Over the course of the past few weeks, he'd fallen woefully behind on of-

fice work. He told himself he'd simply been busy dodging
snowballs and dealing with the grant application paperwork. He refused to admit that his mess of an office had
anything to do with Posy's return to Aurora.

*Keep telling yourself that. Your head has been all over
the place lately.*

He had stacks of permission forms that had never been
filed, the calendar of youth activities required revisions
and the youth department website was sorely in need of
updating. The first two items on his to-do list probably
could have waited, but that last chore probably needed to
be taken care of before their application for the grant was
turned in. It sure couldn't hurt. Given the youth group's
funds, or lack thereof, hiring an actual Webmaster was an
unheard-of luxury. That chore, like so many others, fell
squarely on Liam's shoulders. And there was no time like
the present to get caught up.

He logged on to the hosting site and uploaded a few photos from recent youth-group activities. Within just a few
minutes of getting started, the steady thump-thump of music
drifted toward his office from the fellowship hall.

Liam's fingertips grew still over his keyboard, and he
strained to hear the score. It sounded vaguely familiar.
Something classical, no doubt. Ronnie was probably rolling his eyes right that very second.

Maybe he should go look in on things, just to be sure
Ronnie's attitude stayed in check.

Right. It's Ronnie you want to see.

Liam scowled at his reflection in the computer monitor.
Of course Ronnie was the one he was concerned about.
After all, the kid hadn't seemed all that enthusiastic about
the prospect of dancing in the recital. Liam had pretty
much tricked him into agreeing to participate.

Posy can handle things. Mind your own business.

He went back to jabbing at his keyboard and willed

himself to ignore the music coming from the fellowship hall. Within five minutes, his foot was tapping along to the melody. He continued uploading photos, one after another, and suddenly the music came to an abrupt halt.

His foot grew restless. He waited for the tune to resume. It didn't. He waited, then waited some more. Nothing.

Do not go in there.

Once again, he stared at himself in the glossy screen of his monitor. "You're going in there, aren't you?"

He huffed out a sigh and pushed out of his chair. *You're not spending all afternoon crashing Posy's rehearsal. One minute. Five, tops.*

"Pastor." Ronnie's face grew deep crimson the moment Liam crossed the threshold. His hands, which had been placed gingerly around Melody's waist, jerked away at once. "What are you doing here?"

Melody collapsed out of a tentative-looking arabesque and went teetering face-first toward the floor. Panic gripped Liam by the throat. He'd known all along this was a bad idea. Someone was bound to get hurt. He leaped toward Melody to keep her from falling, but Posy had already steadied her. Liam found himself grasping at nothing but air.

"I've got her. She's fine," Posy said.

Melody beamed up at Posy with an expression of hero worship and wonder on her face that mirrored that of every girl in the youth group lately. They all wanted to be Posy when they grew up. Every last one of them. And by all appearances, Posy adored them with equal affection.

Posy aimed a quizzical look at him over Melody's outstretched arm. "What are you doing here? Besides distracting my danseur, that is."

Ronnie's face grew three shades redder. "Please don't call me that. It sounds dumb."

Melody dropped her extended leg, stood upright and

jammed her hands on her hips. "It means *male dancer* in French. That's all. You're the one being dumb."

Ronnie crossed his arms. "This is your recital, not mine. I'm doing you a favor. The least you could do is be nice."

They were at each other's throats. Already. It had to be some kind of record.

Liam glanced at Posy and lifted a brow. "I thought I'd come check on things. How's it going?"

"You're looking at it." Posy blew a stray wisp of hair from her eyes. "And this is mild compared to earlier."

"So it's going that well, huh?" Liam asked.

"You can't just let go of me like that, Ronnie. Don't you get it? I'll fall over, right in front of the entire town." Melody threw her hands in the air. "Is that what you want?"

"No, b-but…" Ronnie stammered and cast a pleading glance at Liam.

"But what?" Melody wailed.

Liam held up his hands. "Everyone just calm down. Maybe we should take a break for a minute."

We. He had nothing to do with this. He'd been in the room less than three minutes, and now he was talking in terms of *we*.

"We don't have time for a break, Pastor." Melody's lower lip wobbled ever so slightly. Great. She was on the verge of tears.

"She's right." Posy shook her head. "We have an enormous amount of work to do. They've got to learn the entire dance this afternoon if we're going to have time to perfect it before the recital."

"Okay. Well, what exactly seems to be the problem?" he asked. Other than the fact that the two dancers wanted to strangle one another.

"He keeps letting go." Melody shot an accusatory glare at Ronnie. "I think he's doing it on purpose."

"No, I'm not. It's just weird, that's all," Ronnie said. "I thought we'd be dancing."

"We would be, if you'd keep your hands on my waist." Melody pointed at either side of her waist with exaggerated force. Ronnie looked as if he wanted to die.

"Let's try it again, shall we?" Posy smiled, but Liam could see the worry creeping into her expression. "Ronnie, stand here. Right here."

She moved Ronnie by the shoulders until he was standing less than an inch behind Melody.

"Now isn't the time to be shy." She took his hands and planted them on Melody's waist. "If you don't support her, she'll fall. Do you want that?"

If you don't support her, she'll fall.

Liam cleared his throat.

"No, of course not," Ronnie said.

There was hesitation in his posture. Liam could see it. He was afraid. Sure enough, as soon as Posy turned the music back on and Melody stretched into her arabesque, Ronnie's grip on her waist grew more and more tentative. Melody wobbled on tiptoe and nearly spilled onto the floor.

Posy shook her head. "Whatever you do, don't let go of her."

Whatever you do, don't let go of her.

The back of Liam's neck began to perspire.

"I'm not," Ronnie said and somehow managed to keep holding on until Melody straightened upright again. He breathed a visible sigh of relief when both of her feet were back on the floor. "I did it."

He was right. He'd done it. It hadn't been pretty. Or graceful by any stretch of the imagination, but at least no one had ended up facedown on the ground.

"That was good, Ronnie. But I want you to think about something. Pas de deux means *step of two*, and in this dance, each dancer is just as important as the other. The ballerina is usually the dancer who is showcased." She pointed at Melody, who beamed.

Posy continued. "Throughout the dance, the audience will be looking at her graceful arabesque and her beautiful positions. But she can only do these things because you're there, supporting her. Alone, a ballerina can dance beautifully, but with a partner, she can do so much more."

Liam's chest grew tight for some odd reason. He suddenly found it difficult to breathe.

"Her dance partner remains largely in the background, but it's his support that allows her to float across the stage with such beauty. That's why the pas de deux is usually the bravura highlight of a ballet. That's what makes it special. Oftentimes it looks as though the danseur isn't dancing at all, but the ballerina couldn't do what she does without him. Do you understand?"

Ronnie nodded. "I do."

Liam glanced at Posy. Her gaze met his for a prolonged, electrically charged moment before she looked away.

Liam shifted uncomfortably from one foot to the other. He shouldn't be here. This wasn't his world. It never had been, and it never would be. And yet...

Alone, a ballerina can dance beautifully, but with a partner she can do so much more.

Why did he get the feeling that Posy had been talking about far more than a simple dance between two teenagers?

Don't read into things. She's talking about ballet. Nothing more.

"Liam and I will show you. Won't we?" Posy crossed her arms over her wraparound leotard top and raised her eyebrows at him.

He swallowed. "We will?"

Grow up. She's not asking any more of you than you're expecting from Ronnie. And he's a kid.

"Sure." She restarted the music, then took her place back in the center of the room and reached for him. "Come on."

Melody and Ronnie stared at him, waiting. He had no choice. What kind of example would he set if he refused?

Wordlessly, he took his place behind her.

She took his hands in hers and placed them on her waist. Was it his imagination, or was there a slight tremor in her fingertips? "All you have to do is hold on. Got it?"

All you have to do is let me. "Got it."

She leaned forward into a deep arabesque, her left leg rising at an impossibly high angle. Liam kept a firm grip on her waist, steadying her, helping her balance. He could feel her heartbeat through the tips of his fingers, the quickening of her breath in his palms. She lowered her leg and began a series of rapid turns on one foot, spinning through his hands like a top. Round and round, so quickly that Liam lost count of the rotations. Once or twice she lost her center, but his grip quickly righted her, and she kept on going. And going. She didn't stop until the music came to an end.

Then it was over.

Melody and Ronnie burst into applause.

"See, that's how you do it," Melody said. "It was perfect, simply perfect."

"Not quite perfect," Liam muttered, finally finding his voice after a minute or two of breathless confusion. What had just happened?

"Yes." Posy nodded. For a moment, Liam could have sworn he saw tears glistening in her eyes. Then she blinked, and they were gone. "Yes, it was. Perfect. Thank you, Liam."

Don't let go.

His hands felt painfully empty all of a sudden. "You're welcome."

Chapter Sixteen

Posy could scarcely believe it, but things had finally come together. The girls had memorized their dances, the venue was ready, the programs had been printed and the costumes altered by Kirimi at no charge. Even Ronnie had stepped up to the plate, and after the initial disastrous rehearsal, the pas de deux was presentable. It wasn't a masterpiece by any stretch of the imagination, but it would work. Posy was sure of it. The audience would never expect to see a boy onstage, and she'd choreographed a rather grand entrance for him.

By all indications, everything was perfect, and not a moment too soon. The recital was in less than twenty-four hours.

No more dance classes, no more practice, no more rehearsals. They'd had the final dress rehearsal immediately following school. The only thing left to do was get a good night's sleep and show up at the church the next evening to caravan over to the community center where the recital was being held. She was beginning to believe that she could actually pull it off. And what was more, she thought they might even have a chance at winning the grant.

Then why did she have such an uneasy feeling in the pit of her stomach?

Because once the recital is finished, it's all over.

How had five and a half weeks gone by so quickly? She felt as if she'd just touched down on the frozen airstrip behind the Northern Lights Inn. Now she had only three days left until her audition back in San Francisco. The morning after the recital, she'd be sitting on an airplane headed back to her real life.

Real life.

She thought about her lonely apartment back in the city and how she'd never even gotten around to purchasing real plates and bowls since she was often too busy or too tired to cook. Take-out containers worked just fine. She thought about how she'd spent Christmas morning last year alone since she'd had to perform the *The Nutcracker* the night before, and once the show was over, it had been too late to catch a flight to Alaska. She thought about how company class was so quiet that she could hear the swish of each and every pair of ballet slippers as they whispered across the hardwood floor. Then she thought about the laughter of the girls in the youth group, and she thought about Liam and the way he'd spun her around the pond.

Suddenly she couldn't quite figure out which life was real and which one was only temporary.

Don't be ridiculous. You've got a shot at your dream job back in California. The chance to audition for a principal spot doesn't come along every day, or even every year.

Once this was all over, she'd go back to her real life. Everything would go back to the way it had been before. Everything. That included things with Liam. It had to.

Even so, she felt a vague sense of dread hanging in the air as she came home from dress rehearsal. The look on her mother's face when she greeted her in the foyer didn't help matters.

"Where have you been?" she asked. "Gabriel has called here for you three times in the past hour."

"Rehearsal ran late. What do you mean Gabriel called?" There had to be a mistake. Why would Gabriel call her childhood home looking for her? He had her cell number.

Then again, she hadn't exactly been paying attention to her cell phone much lately. She hadn't had time. The recital had completely taken over her life.

"He said he found our number in your paperwork from when you first joined the company. And I have to say, Posy, he didn't sound happy. The *Firebird* auditions are tomorrow afternoon, and he said he still hasn't gotten confirmation of your arrival back in San Francisco." Posy's mom threw her hands in the air. "Did you know about this?"

Panic blossomed in Posy's chest. She couldn't breathe all of a sudden. She needed to sit down. And apparently, she needed to do so in San Francisco, not her childhood living room in Alaska. "I don't understand. The last I heard, the auditions were scheduled for the twenty-fifth. This can't possibly be happening."

God, please. This isn't real. It can't be.
It just can't.

When Liam's doorbell rang right as he was heading to bed, he worried something had happened to one of the kids from youth group. He was unable to think of anyone else who would even call him at that time of night, much less show up on his doorstep. The last person he expected to find on the other side of the door was Posy.

Yet there she stood.

With tears streaming down her face.

"Posy?" He swung the door open wider. "Come in, come in."

She stepped over the threshold, but went no farther. She simply stood there in his entryway, hugging herself and looking as though the bottom had dropped out of her entire world.

Sundog climbed off the sofa and came running the moment he spotted Posy, greeting her in tail-wagging ecstasy. Whatever was wrong, Liam thought such an effusive welcome would cheer her up, even just a fraction. Posy and Sundog had become fast friends after the night Liam had danced with her at the pond. She'd even begun to teach the dog new tricks in addition to the *sit* command, which they'd pretty much perfected during Posy's moments of downtime at the church.

If anything, Sundog's delight upon seeing her only appeared to make her more upset. Liam wondered if something had happened to one of her parents. Or possibly Zoey or Anya. Whatever was wrong, he was glad she'd come to him, even if it felt wholly surreal to see her standing in his house.

It had been the final vestige, past or present. The only part of his life that had been untouched by Posy. She somehow managed to look both as if she belonged there and as if she wasn't actually standing there at all. A vision. A dream.

"Sit down. Please," he said.

Sundog plopped into a sit position.

Liam shook his head. "Not you. Here." He handed Sundog a rawhide chew that was sure to last less than five seconds and pointed toward his dog bed. "Go keep yourself busy."

Sundog snatched the rawhide in his sizable jaws, strolled right past the dog bed and settled himself on the sofa. Naturally. At least he'd ceased gnawing on its cushions.

"Come all the way in and sit down, darling." Liam reached for her hand and gave it a gentle tug.

She shook her head. "Don't. Please don't. Don't hold

my hand, and don't call me darling. This is hard enough. Please don't make it harder by being so nice to me."

He dropped her hand. He still didn't know what had gotten her so upset, but he had the distinct feeling that the bottom was about to drop out of *his* world. Not hers. "Posy, why are you here?"

She took a deep breath. "To say goodbye."

He'd known this was coming. Not a moment went by in which he didn't think about her eventual departure. Every moment of the past five and a half weeks had felt like some sort of angst-ridden countdown.

But why now? She wasn't leaving for three more days. "Posy, let's not do this now. You're not ready. I'm not ready. There will be time for goodbyes."

She wiped at her face. She'd stopped crying, and her expression had turned blank. Emotionless. She looked like a person who was pretending to be someone else. "No, you don't understand. My audition has been rescheduled. I'm leaving tomorrow."

"Tomorrow." But that was impossible. "You can't leave tomorrow. The recital is tomorrow night."

"I know. I hate to miss it, but everything is all set. I'm sure it will go off without a hitch…"

He held up a hand. "Stop. Don't, Posy. Think about what you're saying. You can't do this." *Again.* It took every ounce of self-control he possessed not to say that ugly word. "You can't do this to those girls. They love you. It would break their hearts."

"I don't have a choice. If I don't go, I'll miss the audition and there won't be another one. Maybe ever. This is my career we're talking about."

Ballet, ballet, ballet. Wasn't it what they were *always* talking about?

"But you're dancing *here* tomorrow night. Remember?" He didn't care why she stuck around for the recital, only that she did. He would hang her performance over her head if he had to. He'd get her to stay by whatever means necessary. After the recital, she could go to Timbuktu for all he cared. The girls would be heartbroken if she wasn't alongside them on that community-center stage.

"My variation isn't part of their recital. It's nothing. A tiny solo tacked onto the end. No one will miss me." Her tongue tripped on her last sentence, as if even her physical body knew how profoundly untrue it was.

Everyone would miss her. Not just at the recital, but afterward, too. For days, weeks and months to come. Everyone. Even him.

Especially him.

"Posy..." He shook his head, unwilling, unable to say the one word he most wanted to say.

Stay.

"It's decided, Liam. I'm going. It's out of my hands. You don't understand. I have no choice."

She couldn't have been more wrong. He understood perfectly. "You always have a choice."

Chapter Seventeen

"Are you sure about this?" Zoey asked as she held the door to the cockpit of her tiny plane open for Posy. "Because it's not too late to change your mind."

"I'm sure," Posy said, even though she'd never been less sure of anything in her life.

She'd been heartsick when she'd left Liam's house the night before. Absolutely physically ill. She hadn't slept a wink all night long. Every time she'd closed her eyes, she'd seen that look of bitter disappointment on his face.

The worst part, the very worst, was just how long it had taken that look to make an appearance. She'd expected him to become angry the moment she'd told him the news. He hadn't. Rather than fury, his initial reaction had been one of disbelief. Even after all they'd been through, after the way she'd left and never looked back, he'd been unwilling to believe she would do it again. He'd had faith she would do the right thing and be there for the girls. And it was that faith that had nearly brought her to her knees.

She sat woodenly beside Zoey as she conducted her preflight check. Posy owed her big for making the time to get her to Anchorage so quickly. She'd had a handful of charter flights in the morning and midafternoon, but as soon as her schedule had freed up, she'd made plans to get Posy there. The connection time between when they were due to land in Anchorage and when her commercial flight to San Francisco took off would be tight, but she'd still be able to make it so long as everything went smoothly.

The irony, of course, was that she'd be flying directly over the community center as the recital got under way. She wasn't sure she'd be able to look down. She didn't think she could bear it.

"Zoey, am I doing the right thing?" she asked, holding her dance bag tightly to her chest. Her dance bag had been a security blanket for as long as she could remember. And before her dance bag, it had been her purse, because she'd always kept her pointe shoes nestled safely inside. She knew it was silly, but she liked to have those shoes with her. So in bad times, times when it felt as if she was losing everything, she would always have ballet to hold close to her heart.

"I don't know, Posy. Only you can answer that question." Zoey fastened her clipboard in its place on the center console of the cockpit and grabbed her headset. "How do you feel about leaving? Does it feel right?"

No. It feels wrong.

But that didn't make sense at all. If she didn't show up for her audition, all those years of dance would have been for nothing. Leaving Aurora the first time would have been for nothing.

She couldn't turn back time. Staying now wouldn't change anything that had gone on before. She couldn't change the past.

But she could change the future. Maybe not for her and Liam. He would probably never speak to her again, and if he chose not to, she wouldn't blame him. There had to be a limit to how many times a person was willing to be let down. Whatever that limit was, Posy was certain she'd exceeded it.

It might be too late to change her future with Liam, but it wasn't too late to change the future for the girls. The recital hadn't started yet. She could probably still make it if she hurried.

Don't be silly. The damage is done.

By now, Liam would have told them that she'd left. She was free to pack up her pointe shoes and go.

Wait.

Her pointe shoes. Where were her pointe shoes? The last time she'd seen them, they'd been sitting on a chair at the church with their pink ribbons wrapped snugly around them. Surely she hadn't left them there. She never went anywhere without them.

But she couldn't remember packing them. Not last night. Not this morning.

"My pointe shoes!" she shrieked, ripping open her dance bag and rifling through it. "They're not here."

"What?" Zoey removed her headset. "Is something wrong?"

"I forgot my pointe shoes. They're still at the church." She couldn't believe she'd left them there. How had this happened?

Zoey shrugged. "So? Don't you have a million of those things?"

"Yes, but…"

"But what?"

"You don't think it means something, do you? The fact that I forgot them?" She wasn't sure why she was even asking the question. She already knew the answer. She'd known it all along. "Never mind. I can't go."

"Are you serious?" Zoey asked. Posy couldn't help but notice the smile making its way to her lips.

"Dead serious. I'm sorry, Zoey. I just can't leave. I need

to dance at that recital. I gave my word. I need to be there to fill those shoes." She tugged frantically at the door handle. What if it was too late? What if she couldn't get there in time? She couldn't even go straight to the community center. She'd have to stop by the church to get her shoes and her costume.

"Aren't you forgetting something? How are you planning on getting there? I picked you up earlier, remember?"

"Oh, that's right." She slumped back in her seat.

"Here." Zoey dug around in her pocket and fished out her keys. "Take my car. Don't wait for me. I have to cancel our flight plan and get things settled here."

Posy reached for the keys. "Are you sure you don't mind?"

"Of course I don't mind, but you need to hurry. Go! Now!" She pointed at the door.

Go! Now!

Posy opened the door and went.

The church parking lot was snow-covered and empty when Posy pulled up in Zoey's car. She debated forgoing the stop altogether so she wouldn't miss the start of the recital. She could still be there to support the girls and not dance, but that didn't feel right, either. If she was going to do this, to commit to the recital at the expense of her ballet career, she was going to do it 100 percent.

At the expense of her ballet career.

Since the moment she'd made the decision not to step on that airplane, she'd told herself that this didn't mean the end of her career. It simply meant she wouldn't be promoted. She could still go back to being a soloist if she wanted.

But she couldn't think about that right now. She had a recital to attend. She didn't know what she wanted beyond being there for the girls. Right now she just needed to grab her pointe shoes and her costume and get to the community center.

Of course, she was assuming that Liam hadn't otherwise disposed of her tutu. Burned it, or better yet, fed it to Sundog. She wouldn't have blamed him if he had.

The crushing disappointment in his eyes when she'd told him she was leaving had been excruciating to witness. More painful than anything that could have happened to her physical body. Broken bones couldn't compete with the agony of a broken heart. And her heart had shattered when she'd realized the mistake she'd made. Again.

Almost. You're here now.

She didn't expect him to forgive her. Coming back was too little, too late. But she wanted to do right by the girls. To put them first. Before herself, before ballet. She'd figure out the rest of her future after they'd taken their final curtsies.

She felt strange as she darted across the parking lot. Lighter somehow, as if she could jeté straight to the moon. Odd, considering her life was pretty much in shambles at the moment. Nervous energy bubbled inside her. Like the stage fright she'd always struggled with, only intensified. Even her teeth felt strange, as if she'd bit into something sweet and wonderful.

"Hello?" she called into the empty space, surprised to find the door to the church ajar. Then again, this was Aurora. Land of snow, dancing reindeer and unlocked doors.

One of the girls probably forgot to shut the door behind them in the excitement to get to the recital. A good amount of snowy powder had already blown inside, so she hung her purse on the coatrack and hastily swept the snow back outside with the dual-sided ice scraper/snow-brush tool that was always propped by the door.

She did the best she could with minimal effort. Time was ticking away, and she really wanted to get to the recital before any of the girls went onstage. She tossed the ice scraper back in its place, clicked the door properly closed and hurried in the direction of the fellowship hall.

She paused as she passed Liam's office. The interior was dark and the door stood open, but a shuffling noise came from inside. She lingered for a second or two, and just as she'd convinced herself she was hearing things, the noise started up again. Louder this time. Scraping noises, punctuated by two or three grunts, as though someone was trying to move a desk from one end of the room to the other.

Liam.

Her heart échappéd straight to her throat. She wasn't prepared to see him so soon. The memory of his disappointment was too fresh. She had no idea what to say to him. *I'm sorry* seemed like a good start. Wholly inadequate, but a beginning nonetheless. And perhaps it was better that she apologize to him here, in private, rather than at the crowded community center with chattering girls darting to and fro in fluffy tutus.

Another bumping noise came from inside the office. She leaned closer to the crack in the door. "Liam? It's me, Posy. I changed my mind. I'm back."

There was no response. Just eerie silence as the commotion came to an abrupt end.

"I'm sorry." She swallowed around the lump in her throat. Goodness, this was difficult. More difficult than she'd expected, and she wouldn't have thought that was possible.

Of course, it would have been easier if he'd say something. Anything. Or at the very least look at her.

"Liam, I'm coming in. Okay?" She took a deep breath and pushed the door the rest of the way open, but couldn't see much in the darkened office.

She felt for the light switch next to the doorjamb then

was what hurt the most. He'd let himself down.
God down. He hadn't had the faith to put it all on
and tell her how he felt about her.

ached in his pocket for the car keys and cranked
ne to life. He didn't have much time. Only about
ninutes, but that would be long enough.

lled out of the parking lot, all the while telling
he'd just left the entire youth group behind to go
amounted to nothing more than a fool's errand.
ouldn't seem to stop his foot from pressing down
ccelerator or his hands from turning the steer-
el.

gone. What are you doing?

as following his gut. That was what he was doing.
netic, delusional gut.

s just a feeling, nothing more than the faintest of
s. Some vague, insistent voice that he found diffi-
gnore. Realistically, he knew it was probably sim-
wn wishful thinking. But it was the same nebulous
that he'd heard as a kid when he'd decided to make
his home. The same one that had prompted him to
skating pond. The same one that had caused him
in Posy's purse the night of her accident.

, and look how that particular decision turned out.
asn't remorseful. Not deep down, where it mat-
le never had been. Sad, yes. Back then, he'd been
d when she'd refused to come to the door when he
see her and when she'd stopped taking his calls.
l never been sorry he'd told her parents about the
was the right thing to do. He'd saved her.

problem was that she hadn't wanted to be saved.
one of that mattered anymore. He pushed the past
ady to leave it behind once and for all. Since Posy
n back, he'd been living there. Walking through the
history. Her return had brought everything rush-

flipped it on, and the tiny room was bathed in light. She
blinked, confused at first by what she saw.

No Liam. No one. No human, anyway.

She let out a sigh at the familiar sight of Sundog's wooly
backside sticking out from a large overturned trash can in
the corner. Two other big, similar-looking trash cans had
also been knocked over. At first she couldn't figure out
where they'd all come from, but then she recognized them
as the barriers scattered around the field for his snowball
team's practice.

She rolled her eyes. "Really, Sundog? You're so desperate for food that you're rummaging through wastebaskets
that haven't had anything but snow in them for weeks?
Honestly. I'm disappointed in you. I really am. I thought
you and I had been making some progress. Look at you.
The minute you think I've left Alaska, you're back to your
old tricks. What are you even doing here, anyway? Did
everyone leave you behind?"

She braced herself for an enthusiastic assault of flailing paws and dog slobber, but none was forthcoming. Sundog acted as if he didn't even recognize her. He didn't so
much as wag his tail.

Wait a minute.

She stared at his shaggy form protruding from the trash
can. Horror struck her as she realized that not only was
there no wagging tail, there was no tail at all. Period.

Her breath came in short, desperate gasps. She couldn't
seem to get enough air all of a sudden. Her heart hammered so frantically, she was certain she'd perish from
cardiac arrest before she even had a chance to be eaten.
Blood pumped through her veins so hard she could hear
it pulsing in staccato monosyllables.

Bear...bear...bear...

How could this be happening? It was her homecoming

all over again, only this time it was real. She'd run into a bear in church. Not Liam's maniac dog. A real, actual bear.

Stay quiet. Don't draw any attention to yourself.

She prayed it wasn't too late to sneak quietly out of the office. After all, the bear was still buried waist deep in the trash can. Maybe all that heavy plastic had muffled her voice, and Smokey had missed out on her lecture.

She took a tentative step backward and stumbled into the wall. She'd never been so afraid in her life. Her knees were on the verge of buckling. And then her worst fear at the moment was realized. The creature backed out of the trash can and spun around to face her.

Dark furry face topped with round ears and a long, blond muzzle. Quivering black nose. And a mouthful of teeth—yellowed, pointy and large. So very large.

A bear. Most definitely.

With only thirty minutes before the curtain was to go up on the recital, Liam slipped out of the community center.

The girls were all dressed in their new tutus, Anya was busy helping them with their makeup and the music was ready to go. True to her word, Posy had taken care of every detail before she'd left. Except one. And it had been the most important detail of all.

It had killed him to tell the girls she wouldn't be there to perform. Worse than that, she wouldn't see them dance. Their collective reaction had been one of disbelief. They'd sat cross-legged on the floor of the community center with their bottom lips quivering, suddenly in no hurry to put on the costumes they'd been so excited about for weeks.

Afterward, once he'd given them his best attempt at a "the show must go on" speech, he'd simply needed to get away for a few minutes. The air in the community cen-

ter had become unbearably stuffy, Posy's absence.

He was supposed to be the strong on could lean on. He was their adviser, the friend. Above all, he was their anchor. S count on in a world that could so often s ing. He was supposed to have all the ans

But when Melody had looked at him her chin and tears shining in her eyes ar she would ever see Posy again, he didn't for her. What was he supposed to have sai

He'd said the only truth he'd known. "Po you very much, Melody. She cares about all

It had been a nonanswer. A placeholder. stand-in, when what she really needed was Pos her ballet teacher sitting in that auditorium dance. Or at the very least, an assurance that see her again. And it had killed Liam that he it to her.

He needed to get someplace where he again, where he didn't feel this crushing s his chest. But where?

He sat in his Jeep in the parking lot, n ing to turn on the engine. His breath fogg and his hands grew stiff from the cold, b the numbness. He wished it to penetrat heart, his soul. But it didn't. At the cen the very core of his being, he felt it all. E pain, regret.

Love.

Love, even now. Even after she'd gon left him, left Aurora, left it all behind.

He should have told her how he felt. a difference? Would she have stayed know. And that, more than anything,

ing back, everything he'd thought he'd forgotten. Not just their shared past, but everything that had been going on at the time—graduating from high school, facing the idea of being a nineteen-year-old kid all on his own while his family moved on to the next town, wishing that for once he had a place with four walls and rooms that he recognized that he could call home.

It had been a season of heartbreaking change, but now was the season for a heart-changing break. A break from the events that had occurred so long ago. It was time to leave them in the past, where they belonged. Past time. If he'd been living fully in the present, he would have made things work with Sara. He would keep in touch more with his parents. He would have been able to say the one word to Posy that he'd been unable to utter.

Stay.

He hit every red light between the community center and his destination. At the last one, he nearly gave up on his nonsensical mission and turned around. Right as he was about to jerk the gearshift into Reverse, the light changed. He breezed on through it and turned into the church parking lot.

He didn't expect to see a vehicle in the lot. Particularly not Zoey's car. Didn't she have a flight to Anchorage this afternoon? And wasn't Posy on that flight?

He frowned at the car and tried to shake the feeling that something was wrong. Very wrong. Surely there was a simple explanation. Her flight had probably taken off early or something. Maybe she'd made sure to get back in time to catch the recital. Maybe she'd even pushed her schedule back so Posy could be here to see the girls.

His teeth ground together. Nope. If that were the case, she'd miss her audition altogether. He climbed out of his Jeep, slammed the door and headed inside, unable to shake the nagging feeling that things weren't quite right.

It wasn't until his hand was on the doorknob that he heard the first scream.

No, not a scream exactly. More like a groan. A deep guttural groan that didn't sound quite human. In the eerie silence that followed, the hairs on the back of Liam's neck stood on end. His skin broke out in goose bumps. When the second growl pierced the air, a riot of sensations swelled inside Liam. Not panic, which would have been perfectly logical, but determination. Determination, with a generous dose of anger.

He didn't think, didn't plot or plan. He just ran toward the sounds, which grew louder and more frequent as he dashed in their direction. He skidded around the corner of the hallway and realized they were coming from his office at the end of the corridor, where his door stood open and the light glowed gold.

He could see trash cans knocked over, a dark brown blur, a graceful arm wrapped around the doorjamb and, at the end of that arm, a white-knuckled hand gripping the wood in terror.

Posy.

If he'd paused to take in the scene before him once he reached his office, he would have been paralyzed by fright. But the sight of Posy backed against a wall, mere inches from a large black bear swatting its massive paws at her face and abdomen, barely registered before he started screaming and banging on the door.

"Hey! Get out of here!" he yelled, beating on the door so hard that he heard what sounded like a bone breaking in his hand.

The bear's paw froze midair. He swung his head around to face Liam and snorted. Once, twice, three times. His breath was hot and rancid. Bile rose to the back of Liam's throat.

"I said get out of here!" he yelled again, this time wav-

flipped it on, and the tiny room was bathed in light. She blinked, confused at first by what she saw.

No Liam. No one. No human, anyway.

She let out a sigh at the familiar sight of Sundog's wooly backside sticking out from a large overturned trash can in the corner. Two other big, similar-looking trash cans had also been knocked over. At first she couldn't figure out where they'd all come from, but then she recognized them as the barriers scattered around the field for his snowball team's practice.

She rolled her eyes. "Really, Sundog? You're so desperate for food that you're rummaging through wastebaskets that haven't had anything but snow in them for weeks? Honestly. I'm disappointed in you. I really am. I thought you and I had been making some progress. Look at you. The minute you think I've left Alaska, you're back to your old tricks. What are you even doing here, anyway? Did everyone leave you behind?"

She braced herself for an enthusiastic assault of flailing paws and dog slobber, but none was forthcoming. Sundog acted as if he didn't even recognize her. He didn't so much as wag his tail.

Wait a minute.

She stared at his shaggy form protruding from the trash can. Horror struck her as she realized that not only was there no wagging tail, there was no tail at all. Period.

Her breath came in short, desperate gasps. She couldn't seem to get enough air all of a sudden. Her heart hammered so frantically, she was certain she'd perish from cardiac arrest before she even had a chance to be eaten. Blood pumped through her veins so hard she could hear it pulsing in staccato monosyllables.

Bear...bear...bear...

How could this be happening? It was her homecoming

all over again, only this time it was real. She'd run into a bear in church. Not Liam's maniac dog. A real, actual bear.

Stay quiet. Don't draw any attention to yourself.

She prayed it wasn't too late to sneak quietly out of the office. After all, the bear was still buried waist deep in the trash can. Maybe all that heavy plastic had muffled her voice, and Smokey had missed out on her lecture.

She took a tentative step backward and stumbled into the wall. She'd never been so afraid in her life. Her knees were on the verge of buckling. And then her worst fear at the moment was realized. The creature backed out of the trash can and spun around to face her.

Dark furry face topped with round ears and a long, blond muzzle. Quivering black nose. And a mouthful of teeth— yellowed, pointy and large. So very large.

A bear. Most definitely.

With only thirty minutes before the curtain was to go up on the recital, Liam slipped out of the community center.

The girls were all dressed in their new tutus, Anya was busy helping them with their makeup and the music was ready to go. True to her word, Posy had taken care of every detail before she'd left. Except one. And it had been the most important detail of all.

It had killed him to tell the girls she wouldn't be there to perform. Worse than that, she wouldn't see them dance. Their collective reaction had been one of disbelief. They'd sat cross-legged on the floor of the community center with their bottom lips quivering, suddenly in no hurry to put on the costumes they'd been so excited about for weeks.

Afterward, once he'd given them his best attempt at a "the show must go on" speech, he'd simply needed to get away for a few minutes. The air in the community center had become unbearably stuffy, weighted down with Posy's absence.

He was supposed to be the strong one, someone the kids could lean on. He was their adviser, their cheerleader, their friend. Above all, he was their anchor. Someone they could count on in a world that could so often seem overwhelming. He was supposed to have all the answers.

But when Melody had looked at him with a wobble in her chin and tears shining in her eyes and asked him if she would ever see Posy again, he didn't have an answer for her. What was he supposed to have said?

He'd said the only truth he'd known. "Posy cares about you very much, Melody. She cares about all of us."

It had been a nonanswer. A placeholder. Words as a stand-in, when what she really needed was Posy. She needed her ballet teacher sitting in that auditorium watching her dance. Or at the very least, an assurance that she'd one day see her again. And it had killed Liam that he couldn't give it to her.

He needed to get someplace where he could breathe again, where he didn't feel this crushing sense of loss in his chest. But where?

He sat in his Jeep in the parking lot, not even bothering to turn on the engine. His breath fogged the windows and his hands grew stiff from the cold, but he welcomed the numbness. He wished it to penetrate his bones, his heart, his soul. But it didn't. At the center of himself, at the very core of his being, he felt it all. Everything—loss, pain, regret.

Love.

Love, even now. Even after she'd gone. Even after she'd left him, left Aurora, left it all behind. Again.

He should have told her how he felt. Would it have made a difference? Would she have stayed? He would never know. And that, more than anything, more than even her absence, was what hurt the most. He'd let himself down. He'd let God down. He hadn't had the faith to put it all on the line and tell her how he felt about her.

He reached in his pocket for the car keys and cranked the engine to life. He didn't have much time. Only about twenty minutes, but that would be long enough.

He pulled out of the parking lot, all the while telling himself he'd just left the entire youth group behind to go on what amounted to nothing more than a fool's errand. But he couldn't seem to stop his foot from pressing down on the accelerator or his hands from turning the steering wheel.

She's gone. What are you doing?

He was following his gut. That was what he was doing. His pathetic, delusional gut.

It was just a feeling, nothing more than the faintest of instincts. Some vague, insistent voice that he found difficult to ignore. Realistically, he knew it was probably simply his own wishful thinking. But it was the same nebulous whisper that he'd heard as a kid when he'd decided to make Aurora his home. The same one that had prompted him to buy the skating pond. The same one that had caused him to look in Posy's purse the night of her accident.

Yeah, and look how that particular decision turned out.

He wasn't remorseful. Not deep down, where it mattered. He never had been. Sad, yes. Back then, he'd been shattered when she'd refused to come to the door when he tried to see her and when she'd stopped taking his calls. But he'd never been sorry he'd told her parents about the pills. It was the right thing to do. He'd saved her.

The problem was that she hadn't wanted to be saved.

But none of that mattered anymore. He pushed the past away, ready to leave it behind once and for all. Since Posy had been back, he'd been living there. Walking through the pages of history. Her return had brought everything rushing back, everything he'd thought he'd forgotten. Not just their shared past, but everything that had been going on at the time—graduating from high school, facing the idea of being a nineteen-year-old kid all on his own while his family moved on to the next town, wishing that for once he had a place with four walls and rooms that he recognized that he could call home.

It had been a season of heartbreaking change, but now was the season for a heart-changing break. A break from the events that had occurred so long ago. It was time to leave them in the past, where they belonged. Past time. If he'd been living fully in the present, he would have made things work with Sara. He would keep in touch more with his parents. He would have been able to say the one word to Posy that he'd been unable to utter.

Stay.

He hit every red light between the community center and his destination. At the last one, he nearly gave up on his nonsensical mission and turned around. Right as he was about to jerk the gearshift into Reverse, the light changed. He breezed on through it and turned into the church parking lot.

He didn't expect to see a vehicle in the lot. Particularly not Zoey's car. Didn't she have a flight to Anchorage this afternoon? And wasn't Posy on that flight?

He frowned at the car and tried to shake the feeling that something was wrong. Very wrong. Surely there was a simple explanation. Her flight had probably taken off early or something. Maybe she'd made sure to get back in time to catch the recital. Maybe she'd even pushed her schedule back so Posy could be here to see the girls.

His teeth ground together. Nope. If that were the case, she'd miss her audition altogether. He climbed out of his Jeep, slammed the door and headed inside, unable to shake the nagging feeling that things weren't quite right.

It wasn't until his hand was on the doorknob that he heard the first scream.

No, not a scream exactly. More like a groan. A deep guttural groan that didn't sound quite human. In the eerie silence that followed, the hairs on the back of Liam's neck stood on end. His skin broke out in goose bumps. When the second growl pierced the air, a riot of sensations swelled inside Liam. Not panic, which would have been perfectly logical, but determination. Determination, with a generous dose of anger.

He didn't think, didn't plot or plan. He just ran toward the sounds, which grew louder and more frequent as he dashed in their direction. He skidded around the corner of the hallway and realized they were coming from his office at the end of the corridor, where his door stood open and the light glowed gold.

He could see trash cans knocked over, a dark brown blur, a graceful arm wrapped around the doorjamb and, at the end of that arm, a white-knuckled hand gripping the wood in terror.

Posy.

If he'd paused to take in the scene before him once he reached his office, he would have been paralyzed by fright. But the sight of Posy backed against a wall, mere inches from a large black bear swatting its massive paws at her face and abdomen, barely registered before he started screaming and banging on the door.

"Hey! Get out of here!" he yelled, beating on the door so hard that he heard what sounded like a bone breaking in his hand.

The bear's paw froze midair. He swung his head around to face Liam and snorted. Once, twice, three times. His breath was hot and rancid. Bile rose to the back of Liam's throat.

"I said get out of here!" he yelled again, this time waving his arms above his head in an effort to make himself look as big and intimidating as possible.

"Liam," Posy whimpered. She trembled so hard she could barely speak, and a river of tears ran down her face. "Thank goodness. Is it really you?"

"It's me. Don't worry. Everything is going to be okay." He wasn't sure where the calm assurance in his voice came from.

Please, God, let everything be okay.

The bear still stood between them on all fours. He was so close that Liam could see the tiny red veins in the whites of his eyes, the yellowing of his teeth and the way his nostrils widened with each grunting breath. He panted heavily, sending ripples through his thick, dark fur.

A black bear. Liam sent up a silent prayer of thanks that it wasn't a grizzly. Although he didn't like the idea of any bear being this close to Posy. Period.

He waved his hands over his head again. "Come on. Out you go."

He stamped his feet, beat on the wall until his fists screamed in agony, and finally, *finally*, with a toss of his wooly head, the bear bounded out of the room.

Liam grabbed Posy by the shoulders. "Stay here. Do not move. Understand?"

She nodded.

"Promise me," he said, in as firm of a tone as he could bring himself to use when her bottom lip was trembling and tears were spilling down her porcelain cheeks.

She was seriously shaken up. But she was still Posy, which meant she was also seriously stubborn. Liam wouldn't be able to turn his back on her if he thought she wasn't safely shut inside the office.

"I promise," she said, her voice no more than a soft, shuddering whisper.

He'd never seen her this afraid. Not even after the accident all those years ago.

He wiped the tears from her cheeks with a gentle swipe of his thumb. "I'll be right back. I've got to make sure our furry friend is out of the church and long gone. Okay?"

"Okay." She gave him a shaky smile. "Please be careful. Please."

"I will. I promise."

"And Liam." She leveled her gaze at him. There were endless storms brewing in her gray eyes. He wondered if he'd ever be able to find the calm in the center of all that chaos. "Thank you."

He said nothing in return. There were too many unspoken words floating between them. Instead, he cupped her cheek and pressed a tender kiss to her forehead.

He wanted nothing more than to bury his hands in her hair, to hold on to her with all his might. He wanted to examine every inch of her to make sure the bear hadn't hurt her. He wanted to make corny jokes until she laughed again.

With more than a little reluctance, he released his hold on her. He grabbed a ruler from his desk, along with one of the overturned trash cans, and turned to go.

Then right as he shut the door to seal Posy inside, he could have sworn he heard her voice, a delicate whisper: "I love you."

Chapter Eighteen

When the door closed behind Liam, the last shred of Posy's composure fell away and her knees buckled. She slid down the wall, wrapped her arms around her legs and stayed wound in a tight ball as she listened to Liam chase the bear out of the building.

Please, God. Don't let him get hurt. I can't lose him. Not like this.

She should have insisted he stay in the office with her. They could have locked themselves in and called the police. Or wildlife control. Or whomever people called when they were being held hostage by bears.

It was all so surreal. Even when those huge paws had been inches away from her face, she couldn't quite believe she'd been trapped in Liam's office with a bear. And her purse, cell phone…everything…were in the other room, still on the table where she'd tossed them when she entered the building. She'd been even less prepared than the time she'd mistaken Sundog for a grizzly. At least then she'd had hair spray.

Although now that she'd actually been in close contact with a bear, she doubted Aqua Net would have accomplished a thing. Other than making the bear remarkably well coiffed. And angry. Very, very angry.

Out in the hallway, Liam banged away on the trash can with his ruler and yelled at the bear. He didn't sound at all afraid, which she found both impressive and immensely reassuring. With each passing second, her heartbeat slowed. The shaking in her hands subsided, as the commotion grew more and more faint. She concentrated on inhaling and exhaling, on controlling her adrenaline, like she tried to do before a performance. Finally, after what felt like an eternity but what was in all probability no more than a minute or two, she heard the door of the church slam shut.

She scrambled to her feet and turned the knob just as Liam pushed the office door open.

"Going somewhere?" he asked, raising a brow. "I thought I told you to stay put."

She was so glad to see him in one piece that she threw her arms around him and buried her face in the crook of his neck. He smelled so good, so familiar. Like evergreens and snowdrifts. Like everything Alaskan.

Like home.

She held him even tighter and blinked back a fresh wave of tears.

"Hey." He pulled back and tipped her chin upward with a touch of his finger so she had no choice but to look directly into his eyes. "The bear is gone. It's over. We're okay."

We're okay.

If only that were true.

She slipped out of his grasp and crossed her arms so she wouldn't be tempted to throw them around his neck again. He'd saved her from being mauled, but that didn't mean he'd been happy to see her. He probably hated her. She'd turned her back on him, on the youth group, on the whole town.

She cleared her throat. "Is Smokey really gone?"

"Smokey?" The corner of his mouth quirked up into a half grin. "You named the bear?"

"Well, you know, I figured if he was going to make a meal out of me, we should be on a first-name basis."

"The bear—*Smokey*, as you so affectionately call him—is gone. He's probably diving in a Dumpster somewhere on Main Street. I called the police and they're out looking for him now."

"That's good." She took another deep breath. She still couldn't seem to get enough air. "That's very good."

He narrowed his gaze at her, studying her, as though he were trying to peer inside her head. "I thought you'd left."

"I did. I mean I almost did. But I couldn't miss the recital. Not after the girls worked so hard. I just couldn't." *And you. I couldn't bear the thought of disappointing you again.*

She needed to tell him. She needed to put it all on the line. "Liam, I…"

He cut her off before she could utter another syllable. "The recital! I almost forgot! What time is it?"

The time. She'd completely lost track of the time.

She'd assumed that since Liam was at the church, the show hadn't begun. Surely the girls weren't onstage right now, while she and Liam were both here. "I don't know. I don't have my phone."

"We need to go. Right now," he said, sounding only slightly less panicked than she'd been when confronted by the bear.

"My shoes. My costume." She waved a hand toward the fellowship hall.

"Right. Okay, you go grab your things. I've got something I need to get loaded up anyway. I'll meet you outside?"

"Sure." She hurried toward the fellowship hall, and

there were her pointe shoes, right where she'd left them. And there was her costume, hanging from the coatrack in its pristine black garment bag with the West Coast Arts Ballet Company logo stamped in gold letters.

When Posy had made that second call to Martha, the costume mistress with the company, she'd simply asked if there was anything available to borrow. Anything at all in her size, or close to her size. She'd safety pin something in place if necessary. She'd known how excited the girls would be to see a real, professional ballet costume. There were racks upon racks of old tutus backstage. Heavily beaded bodices, diaphanous tulle skirts, rhinestone tiaras that glittered like diamonds as ballerinas floated between light and shadow onstage.

Martha had always been fond of Posy. In truth, she was probably the only person in California whom Posy could call a friend. There was no undercurrent of competition to get in the way between them. And unlike the other dancers, Posy didn't look right through her.

Martha had assured Posy she'd do what she could. She knew Posy's measurements like the back of her hand. The garment bag had arrived the very same afternoon as the message from Gabriel. Posy hadn't even bothered to open it. And here it hung, right where she'd left it.

The difference was that now it was probably the last such costume she'd ever wear.

Stop. You can still go back as a soloist.

Of course she could. Probably. Maybe. So long as Gabriel wasn't furious when she failed to turn up for the audition as promised.

But was that what she wanted?

This isn't the time to figure out your career. You've got a show to put on. It's time to dance.

Time to dance.

Here. In Alaska. With Liam sitting in the audience.

When she'd left so long ago, she'd never imagined something like this would happen. It felt like the second chance she'd never had the courage to hope for.

She grabbed the garment bag. Curiosity got the best of her, and she peeked inside.

Just a tiny, quick glance.

A fleeting glimpse was all it took. She recognized the white confection with the glass beads and silver lace bodice at once. This was no spare costume that had been hanging backstage for a decade. Martha had sent her the Winter Fairy costume from *Cinderella*, the tutu she'd been wearing when she'd gotten injured.

Posy could hardly believe she'd been entrusted with such a treasure. It was the prettiest costume she'd ever worn. But even better, it meant she could finish what she'd started. Wearing it today would be poetic. Another chance at her final dance.

She held the garment bag to her heart as she rushed back to Liam's office. He wasn't there. Then she remembered he'd told her that he would meet her outside so they could ride to the recital together. He'd mentioned needing to load something up in his car. She'd been so rattled in the wake of her run-in with Smokey that she hadn't even asked him what that something might be.

Now that she thought about it, she didn't know why he was at the church at all. Why wasn't he at the community center with everyone else? It wasn't like Liam to leave the youth group, much less in the final minutes before the big recital. Exactly what was he doing here?

Other than saving her life and all.

Liam sat in the audience at the community center and did his best to pay attention to what was happening onstage. He didn't want to miss a moment of it. The girls had been so happy to see Posy that the smiles on their faces were 100 percent genuine. Gone were the butterflies and the panicked bouts of stage fright. The teenagers were filled with the joy of an unexpected blessing, and it showed in every pointed toe and graceful arm.

Melody and Ronnie's pas de deux brought the house down. Posy had been right all along. No one expected to see a boy onstage. When he walked out, extended his arm with a flourish and bowed deeply to Melody, an audible gasp had passed through the audience. Their dance was simple, sweet. Melody stood on tiptoe and extended her graceful skater's limbs in a variety of poses while Ronnie held her by the hand. Their grand finale came when he wrapped an arm around her waist and guided her in a series of rapid turns that ended in perfect time to the music. Beside Liam, two women he recognized from the knitting group that met at the church on Monday nights clapped and loudly exclaimed that they'd forgotten they'd been watching kids from the youth group. They felt as though they'd been to a real performance, which was of course what Posy had wanted all along.

As remarkable as it was, Liam sat through the majority of the evening in a daze. He felt as though he were moving in slow motion, and all the activity around him was taking place at warp speed. He wanted to slow it down so he could take it all in.

The truth of the matter was that he was only halfway paying attention to the outside world. On the exterior, he was smiling when he should and clapping at all the appropriate moments. On the inside, however, a fit of emotion held sway.

Posy had said she loved him.

She hadn't said it directly, and it had been uttered in the softest of whispers, but he'd heard it.

I love you.

They were the words Liam had waited to hear since the

night he'd broken her heart. Words that he'd thought had been forever washed away by the tragic rain.

As much as he wanted to claim those words, he couldn't. She'd been upset. She'd nearly been mauled. She was grateful. Nothing more.

But part of him held out hope it was more than that.

She'd come back. She'd left, just as he'd known she would all along. Just as she had before. But this time had been different. This time she'd come back.

And now he sat with those three magic words still echoing in his head as he watched her take center stage in a cloud of white tulle and shoes of the palest pink satin. She was breathtaking, from the dazzling diamond tiara that sat atop her flame of red hair to the tips of her elegant fingers. He'd seen her dance before, of course. Years ago. But it was clear that in her years away, her artistry had matured into a thing of heartbreaking beauty. She could tell an entire story with just the turn of her wrist. And Liam wanted to memorize every word.

He forgot how to breathe when she rose up en pointe and extended one supple leg in a spellbinding attitude devant. And when she exploded in a series of rapid pas de chats, he could have sworn he felt every strike of her foot dead in the center of his chest. As if she'd somehow leaped into the very center of his being.

Don't let her go.

When she'd finished, when the audience members had risen to their feet all around him, Liam had been the only one to remain sitting. He didn't trust his legs to stand.

Josephine Sutton had swept him clear off his feet.

Posy was mobbed with well-wishers at the end of the recital. Lou McNeil, her parents, teenagers from the skating rink, patrons of the Northern Lights Inn coffee bar,

Zoey and Anya, along with their husbands. And of course, the kids from the youth group.

The girls were on the verge of tears and didn't seem to understand whether they were crying from joy or sorrow. The entire experience had overwhelmed them, grabbed them each by the throat. They were too young and naive to realize what was happening, but Posy knew.

Years from now, whether they found themselves sitting in the red velvet interior of a theater or, by some balletic twist of fate, they were the ones dancing onstage, each of them would look back on this day, this moment. And they would recognize it as the day they'd fallen in love with ballet.

She almost envied them. Almost. Just as she'd almost envied Melody when Ronnie had asked her to be his date for the school prom in the moment the closing curtain fell.

So many people. Anywhere and everywhere. Posy had never been mobbed like this after a performance. But as nice as it felt to hear praise for the work she'd done with the girls, there was only one person whom she truly wanted to see. One person whose opinion mattered.

"Zoey, have you seen Liam?" Posy asked when she spotted her friend making her way through the crowd with a tray of paper cups.

"Oh, hi! Would you like a White Swan Mocha?" She offered Posy a cup.

The Northern Lights Inn coffee bar had generously donated refreshments for the evening. Posy, Zoey and Anya had taste-tested a variety of offerings they'd concocted for the event, ranging from the White Swan Mocha to the Black Swan Chocolate Latte. Posy would never look at coffee the same way she had prior to her return to Aurora.

"No, thanks." Posy shook her head. "I need to talk to Liam. Do you know where he is?"

"I think I saw him head outside a few minutes ago." She pointed toward the side door.

Outside? What was he doing out in the snow? "I'm going to go look for him. If anyone needs me, just tell them I'll be right back, okay?"

"Wait. Won't your shoes get ruined?" She glanced at Posy's feet, still clad in pink satin and ribbons. "Let me find a place to put this tray, and I'll help you get changed."

"That's okay. I really need to talk to him. It's important."

"Okay." Zoey winked. "Go get him."

Go get him.

She made it sound so easy, when in reality Posy still didn't know if he'd forgiven her for leaving. Again.

Please, God.

She pushed through the door and out into the cold. Evening had arrived early, as it always did this time of year in Aurora. The sky stretched overhead in an expanse of black velvet, and it had just barely begun to snow. A snowfall so soft and gentle it almost didn't look real, but rather like the fake snow that fell from the rafters during *Nutcracker* season.

But Posy knew better. There was nothing artificial about this snowfall, nor was there anything artificial about her feelings. That was one of the best things about Alaska—its authenticity. Everything was real here. She couldn't hide, and she'd come to realize that was exactly what she'd been doing in San Francisco. It was the reason she'd never come home.

She'd convinced herself she'd simply wanted to dance when, in reality, she'd been running. She didn't want to run anymore. It was time to start dancing in place.

A shiver coursed through her, and the wind skittered across her bare shoulders. She wrapped her arms around the sparkling bodice of her tutu and headed toward the parking lot.

Moisture seeped through the thin satin heels of her pointe shoes, reminding her of the pair she'd once lost to the rain. She'd gone through countless ballet shoes since that night. The company gave her a new pair for every performance. But of all the shoes she'd ever had, the only ones she'd never been able to bring herself to part with had been that muddied pair. They'd been her last link to Liam.

She tiptoed through the slush on demi pointe until she spotted Liam walking toward her from the crowded parking lot. In one arm he carried what looked like a suitcase, which didn't make sense at all. In the other, he held what amounted to a pound of gold this far from the Lower 48—an enormous bouquet of red roses.

"Posy," he said, his eyes widening as he took in the sight of her. A ballerina in the snow. "You're going to freeze to death. What are you doing out here?"

"Looking for you." He was wrong. She wasn't anywhere close to freezing to death. Just the sight of him sent a wave of warmth washing over her. "Nice roses. I'm guessing they're for the girls?"

"No, actually. I got pink ones for the girls. Zoey flew them in for me yesterday. They're backstage." He held the roses toward her. "These are for you."

She gathered the bouquet in her arms. Snowflakes danced against the crimson petals, a kiss of innocence.

"For me? All of them?" There had to be at least three or four dozen, an unheard-of extravagance in Alaska. "You didn't have to do that, Liam."

"Who said I had to? I wanted to." He sounded oddly serious for someone talking about roses. "You were beautiful tonight, Posy. There aren't enough roses in the world to tell you what a beautiful dancer you are."

"Liam…"

"But maybe this will." He gestured toward the suitcase in his hands.

Upon closer inspection, it wasn't a suitcase after all. She gasped when she realized what she was looking at—a beat-up blue foldable case for a turntable. Not just any turntable. "Madame Sylvie's record player. How did you know?"

Liam shrugged. "After our night at the skating pond and hearing about your excursion to the thrift shop from Alec, I sort of put two and two together. I'd forgotten it at the church earlier, so I went back to fetch it. That's when I found you and Smokey."

Our night at the skating pond.

"But I'd already told you I was leaving. Why would you go back for the record player? You couldn't possibly know I'd come back. I didn't even know I would." As much as she adored what he was saying, it didn't make sense.

"Maybe I had a little more faith in you than you did in yourself," he said solemnly.

That was all the logic she needed.

For the first time since she'd made the decision to stay, hope stirred in her soul. Then Liam spoke again, and her hopes were promptly dashed. "Take it back to California with you. Maybe then Alaska won't seem so far away. Besides, you need it to play your *Peter and the Wolf* album."

He was joking. At a time like this. Posy couldn't help smiling despite the way her heart felt as though it was on the verge of breaking all over again. Scars upon scars. New and old.

"I came back, remember?"

"But not for good." It was a statement, not a question.

Posy wanted to scream *no* all the same. "You don't want me to stay?"

"I never said that. I want very much for you to stay. I want to fall to my knees right here in the snow and beg you to never set foot out of this town again. I want you to teach every kid in the state of Alaska to dance. I want to save you from bears and marauding dogs. I want to take you skating at the place where we skated as kids. I want to see the winter wind in your hair every day until I stop breathing. I want to kiss you under our tree. I want to marry you in the church where you maced me." He paused, and Posy couldn't help but wonder why he wasn't smiling. She was smiling all the way down to her pointed toes.

Until he finished. "But this isn't about me. It's not about what I want. It's about what you want. What you deserve. And you deserve to dance, Posy. You deserve to dance wherever you want, whether that's California or on the surface of the moon. I can't take that away from you. I can't, and I won't."

If he thought he was getting rid of her that easily, he'd better think again. "But what if I want to dance right here? What if I want to come home?"

He stared at her long and hard, as if he didn't quite believe what she'd just said. "It's your choice, Posy. I'm not a kid anymore. Neither are you. It's time we get this right. I want whatever—*wherever*—makes you happy."

You always have a choice.

"Home is what makes me happy." She could say that now. With complete confidence.

She wouldn't have been able to utter those words six years ago. She'd needed to leave, to run away, if only to appreciate everything and everyone she'd been running from.

"Home?" Liam stepped toward her, wrapped his arms around her waist and pulled her close. She could have stayed right there forever in her tutu in the snow, wrapped in the rose-scented embrace of the man she'd loved since she was just a girl. "Where is home exactly?"

"Here." She rested her hand on his chest and felt the pounding strength of his pulse. It beat in the most glorious of rhythms, a cadence she could never grow tired of dancing to. "Not California. Not Alaska. You. You're my home, Liam. It's always been you."

Yukon Reporter
News from the Last Frontier

March 27

Aurora Youth Program Awarded Grant
by reporter Ben Grayson

The after-school youth ministry at Aurora Community Church was awarded a substantial monetary grant from the state of Alaska this week. Chosen from among over one hundred applicants, the youth program was selected for the award based on the work of ballet dancer and Aurora native Posy Sutton. Working in partnership with youth pastor Liam Blake, Miss Sutton established an instructional ballet program at the church, which caught the eye of the state government with a dance recital featuring her students. According to Pastor Blake, funds from the grant will be used to purchase computers and learning equipment for the youth ministry, in addition to winter clothing items, which will be donated to families in need in the remote village of Kivalina in the Arctic Circle.

Miss Sutton has left the youth ministry at Aurora Community Church in order to open the Sylvie Martin Dance Conservatory, a studio to be devoted to dance education in downtown Aurora. Pastor Blake remains on staff at the church, where the two will be married this summer.

* * * * *

Dear Reader,

Welcome back to Aurora, Alaska!

This book has been a long time coming. I love dance, and for a while now, I've wanted to write a story with a ballerina heroine. I just had to figure out how to get her to Alaska, so I decided to make this a book about coming home.

Homecomings can be bittersweet even under the best of circumstances. When you throw in a career-threatening injury, a bear, an enormous dog and a former high school sweetheart, things get hopelessly complicated. But those are only the start of Posy's problems. What she struggles with most on these pages is the very concept of home, of where she belongs. I think that is a struggle that everyone can understand. But even amid confusion and an uncertain future, God always gives us time to dance.

If this is your first trip to the winter wonderland of Aurora, Alaska, I hope you'll go back and read the other books in this series, *Alaskan Hearts*, *Alaskan Hero* and *Sleigh Bell Sweethearts*.

Until next time. As always, thank you so much for reading!

Teri Wilson

REQUEST YOUR FREE BOOKS!

2 FREE INSPIRATIONAL NOVELS
PLUS 2
FREE
MYSTERY GIFTS

Love Inspired

YES! Please send me 2 FREE Love Inspired® novels and my 2 FREE mystery gifts (gifts are worth about $10). After receiving them, if I don't wish to receive any more books, I can return the shipping statement marked "cancel." If I don't cancel, I will receive 6 brand-new novels every month and be billed just $4.74 per book in the U.S. or $5.24 per book in Canada. That's a saving of at least 21% off the cover price. It's quite a bargain! Shipping and handling is just 50¢ per book in the U.S. and 75¢ per book in Canada.* I understand that accepting the 2 free books and gifts places me under no obligation to buy anything. I can always return a shipment and cancel at any time. Even if I never buy another book, the two free books and gifts are mine to keep forever.

105/305 IDN F47Y

Name _____ (PLEASE PRINT)

Address _____ Apt. #

City _____ State/Prov. _____ Zip/Postal Code

Signature (if under 18, a parent or guardian must sign)

Mail to the Harlequin® Reader Service:
IN U.S.A.: P.O. Box 1867, Buffalo, NY 14240-1867
IN CANADA: P.O. Box 609, Fort Erie, Ontario L2A 5X3

**Are you a subscriber to Love Inspired books
and want to receive the larger-print edition?
Call 1-800-873-8635 or visit www.ReaderService.com.**

* Terms and prices subject to change without notice. Prices do not include applicable taxes. Sales tax applicable in N.Y. Canadian residents will be charged applicable taxes. Offer not valid in Quebec. This offer is limited to one order per household. Not valid for current subscribers to Love Inspired books. All orders subject to credit approval. Credit or debit balances in a customer's account(s) may be offset by any other outstanding balance owed by or to the customer. Please allow 4 to 6 weeks for delivery. Offer available while quantities last.

Your Privacy—The Harlequin® Reader Service is committed to protecting your privacy. Our Privacy Policy is available online at www.ReaderService.com or upon request from the Harlequin Reader Service.

We make a portion of our mailing list available to reputable third parties that offer products we believe may interest you. If you prefer that we not exchange your name with third parties, or if you wish to clarify or modify your communication preferences, please visit us at www.ReaderService.com/consumerschoice or write to us at Harlequin Reader Service Preference Service, P.O. Box 9062, Buffalo, NY 14269. Include your complete name and address.

LI13R

Can Mary find happiness with a secretive stranger who saves her life?

Read on for a sneak preview of the final book in Patricia Davids's
BRIDES OF AMISH COUNTRY *series,*
AMISH REDEMPTION.

Hannah edged closer to her. "I don't like storms."

Mary slipped an arm around her daughter. "Don't worry. We'll be at Katie's house before the rain catches us."

It turned out she was wrong. Big raindrops began hitting her windshield. A strong gust of wind shook the buggy and blew dust across the road. The sky grew darker by the minute. She urged Tilly to a faster pace. She should have stayed home.

A red car flew past her with the driver laying on the horn. Tilly shied and nearly dragged the buggy into the fence along the side of the road. Mary managed to right her. "Foolish *Englischers*. We are over as far as we can get."

The rumble of thunder became a steady roar behind them. Tilly broke into a run. Hannah began screaming. Mary glanced back and her heart stopped. A tornado had dropped from the clouds and was bearing down on them. Dust and debris flew out from the wide base.

Dear God, help me save my baby. What do I do?

She saw an intersection up ahead.

Bracing her legs against the dash, she pulled back on the lines, trying to slow Tilly enough to make the corner without overturning. The mare seemed to sense the plan. She slowed and made the turn with the buggy tilting on two wheels. Mary grabbed Hannah and held on to her. Swerving wildly behind the horse, the buggy finally came back onto all four wheels. Before the mare could gather speed again, a man jumped into the road waving his arms. He grabbed Tilly's bridle and pulled her to a stop.

Shouting, he pointed toward an abandoned farmhouse. "There's a cellar on the south side."

Mary jumped out of the buggy and pulled Hannah into her arms. The man was already unhitching Tilly, so Mary ran toward the ramshackle structure. The wind threatened to pull her off her feet. The trees and even the grass were straining toward the approaching tornado. She reached the old cellar door, but couldn't lift it against the force of the wind. She was about to lie on the ground on top of Hannah when the man appeared at her side. Together, they were able to lift the door.

A second later, she was pushed down the steps into darkness.

Don't miss
AMISH REDEMPTION by Patricia Davids,
available April 2015 wherever
Love Inspired® books and ebooks are sold.

www.Harlequin.com

SPECIAL EXCERPT FROM

Love Inspired **HISTORICAL**

*On the wagon train out West, will Ben Hewitt find love
again with Abigail Bingham Black—the woman who
broke his heart six years ago?*

Read on for a sneak preview of Linda Ford's
WAGON TRAIN REUNION,
the exciting beginning of the new series
JOURNEY WEST.

Benjamin Hewitt stared. It wasn't possible.

The man struggling with his oxen couldn't be
Mr. Bingham. He would never subject himself and his
wife to the trials of this journey. Why, Mrs. Bingham
would look mighty strange fluttering a lace hankie and
expecting someone to serve her tea.

The man must have given the wrong command
because the oxen jerked hard to the right. The rear wheel
broke free. A flurry of smaller items fell out the back. A
woman followed, shrieking.

"Mother, are you injured?" A young woman ran
toward her mother. She sounded just like Abigail. At least
as near as he could recall. He'd succeeded in putting that
young woman from his mind many years ago.

She glanced about. "Father, are you safe?"

The sun glowed in her blond hair and he knew without
seeing her face that it was Abigail. What was she doing
here? She'd not find a fine, big house nor fancy dishes

and certainly no servants on this trip.

The bitterness he'd once felt at being rejected because he couldn't provide those things had dissipated, leaving only regret and caution.

She helped her mother to her feet and dusted her skirts off. All the while, the woman—Mrs. Bingham, to be sure—complained, her voice grating with displeasure that made Ben's nerves twitch. He knew all too well that sound. Could recall in sharp detail when the woman had told him he was not a suitable suitor for her daughter. Abigail had agreed, had told him, in a harsh dismissive tone, she would no longer see him.

It all seemed so long ago. Six years to be exact. He'd been a different person back then. Thanks to Abigail, he'd learned not to trust everything a woman said. Nor believe how they acted.

But Binghams or not, a wheel needed to be put on. Ben joined the men hurrying to assist the family.

"Hello." He greeted Mr. Bingham and the man shook his hand. "Ladies." He tipped his hat to them.

"Hello, Ben." Abigail Bingham stood at her mother's side. No, not Bingham. She was Abigail Black now.

Don't miss
WAGON TRAIN REUNION by Linda Ford,
available April 2015 wherever
Love Inspired® Historical books and ebooks are sold.

www.Harlequin.com